BATTLE STATIONS

By Craig DiLouie

BATTLE STATIONS

A NOVEL OF THE PACIFIC WAR

CRAIG DILOUIE

BATTLE STATIONS
A novel of the Pacific War
©2016 Craig DiLouie. All rights reserved.

Lyrics from "You're a Grand Old Flag" are by George M. Cohan, which he wrote in 1906 for his stage musical, *George Washington, Jr.* (public domain). A line in Chapter 5 is quoted from *Woman of the Year* (1942), produced by Metro-Goldwyn Mayer, under fair-use guidelines. Percy's first quote in Chapter 10 is an ancient proverb. His second quote is from *Inferno*, part one of the *Divine Comedy* written by Dante Alighieri (public domain). Lyrics from "For He's a Jolly Good Fellow" are also in the public domain.

Editing by Timothy Johnson.
Cover art by Eloise Knapp Design.
Book layout by C. Marshall Publishing

Published by ZING Communications, Inc.

www.CraigDiLouie.com

CHAPTER ONE

ATTACK TRAINER

"Start the attack!" Charlie cried. "Up periscope!"

He swept the horizon for Japanese ships, spotted them. The enemy advanced under his crosshairs.

What he saw didn't add up. "Down scope."

The officers watched him. Lt. Grayson, assistant approach officer. Lt. Boyd at the plotting table. Lt. Rohm standing at the torpedo data computer, or TDC.

Shooting a mobile target from a moving submarine involved complex geometry. The crew fed variables such as speed, bearing, and angle on the bow into the TDC. The TDC then produced a torpedo-firing angle. Each time, the problem allowed a small margin of error.

This particular problem would give him almost no margin at all.

"Well?" Grayson asked him.

"Target, bearing two-five-oh," Charlie said. "Oh-two-five on the starboard bow. Range, about 12,000 yards. Give him twelve knots."

To submariners, there were only two kinds of ships,

submarines and targets. A jealous breed, they referred to their own submarine as a "she." Every other ship was a "he."

Charlie added, "He has three escorts screening him. *Asashio*-class destroyers."

The assistant approach officer whistled. "All that protection for one ship? What's the target, Hirohito's yacht?"

Boyd dropped the thick *Reference Book of Japanese Merchant Ships* on the table. Its pages provided valuable information such as tonnage, height above the waterline, and distance from the waterline to the keel, or draft.

Charlie flipped through it and pointed. "I think that's the ship."

A fishing trawler.

Boyd and Rohm exchanged an amused glance.

Grayson's lips curled into a smirk. "You caught a real high-value target, Harrison."

The officers cracked grins. Charlie turned and threw "Quiet Bill" Hutchison, who stood in a corner, a questioning look.

As usual, the old commander's placid expression told him nothing.

"Wait a minute." Charlie pulled out the reference on Imperial Japanese Navy warships and flipped through it. "Yeah. That's it there."

Kinesaki class, 900 tons. Assigned to resupply operations with the China Area Fleet, it hauled eighty tons of frozen food and sixty tons of fresh water. The hull-mounted freezer carried fish, which explained why it looked like a trawler.

Today, it transported something important to the Japanese Empire. Cargo worth three tough DDs, or destroyers, to guard it.

The supply ship lay 200 feet in length, about half as long as the Asashios and two-thirds as long as *Sabertooth*, Charlie's last command. Infiltrating the fast-moving escorts to hit such a small target posed a hell of a challenge.

Rohm read the stats. "Bad luck, Harrison. A real doozy."

No kidding. Their teacher had thrown him a curveball for his last time in the attack trainer, which simulated submarine combat.

The men fought in a dummy conning tower with a fixed periscope that piped into a room upstairs. There, operators worked a system of circular discs connected by control cables. Model ships rode these traveling turntables along a course Quiet Bill set up.

The goal was to approach the target while avoiding detection, fire a straight bow shot, and escape. While a simulation, it felt realistic. As for the stakes, they were very much real.

Tomorrow, Charlie graduated from Prospective Executive Officer School. With more candidates than boats, some got detailed, some didn't.

He shot another glance at Quiet Bill. The commander's eyes appeared to smile at him.

Grayson: "What do you want to do, Harrison?"

"Battle stations, torpedo," Charlie said. "We're going to sink the bastard."

CHAPTER TWO

NEEDLE AND THREAD

The shortened periscope protruded only far enough to offer a view level with the floor. The model ships advanced steadily across the metal sea.

"Supply ship," Charlie said. "Bearing, mark!"

Grayson called out the bearing ring reading on the other side of the periscope shaft. Rohm fed the number into the TDC.

"Range, give him 11,000 yards."

He brought down the periscope. If a commander kept the scope up longer than seven seconds, the operators threw a blanket over it to let him know the Japanese spotted him. Then they gleefully stomped the steel floor to simulate depth charges or airplane bombs.

After a few minutes, he scoped the escorts and repeated the exercise.

The model ships started on one side of the room and stopped at the far side. He knew they headed west by southwest. He didn't know whether they'd maintain this direction and for how long. The targets might zig any time.

Maybe they wouldn't zig at all.

Charlie needed to figure their base course. This required frequent periscope checks. He decided to maintain his own course a bit longer. He had time.

"Come left?" Grayson prompted.

"Steady as you go," Charlie said.

When Grayson took his turn as commander, he bounded after the enemy like a puppy. Sometimes, it worked, but not always. The room overhead represented 200 square miles of open sea. A skipper had to creep within 2,000 yards to hit his target with any accuracy.

Charlie's submarine traveled at a top speed of nine knots. A pace the boat could keep up for only an hour, as it drained her batteries.

He ordered the scope raised again. Called out bearings and ranges.

The supply ship had zigged to the southeast, now bearing 137° True.

The destroyers continued to circle it in their defensive pattern, but he remained focused on the Kinesaki. The supply ship would tell him the group's base course.

One more zig would do it. Then he'd maneuver into a firing position and shoot, assuming the Japanese maintained their course.

"We could nudge northwest," Grayson suggested.

He might be right.

These exercises simulated the challenges of command. The commander, meanwhile, brought his own personal pressures. Grayson, with his movie-star good looks and New England navy family, needed to prove himself.

Charlie felt a similar need. He'd only served in two war patrols and had gotten fast-tracked. He had plenty to prove.

Lt. Commander J.R. Kane had taught him patience, however. Kane viewed undersea combat as a game of chess. You had to wait for the right move.

"Steady on zero," he said.

On the next periscope check, the Kinesaki veered again.

"I've got a base course," Boyd announced in his South Carolina drawl. He laughed. "I'll be damned."

Charlie joined him at the plotting table. "What's funny?"

"They're coming right at us. The target will cross our bow right about here. We really don't have to do anything except hold course."

The officers leaned on the table and studied the plot.

"The distance to the track is 3,000 yards." Boyd tapped the plot with his pencil. "We shoot our fish here at a thousand yards. Like shootin' a barn."

Not quite so easy with a target that small, but Charlie took his point.

Quiet Bill was testing his nerve. He knew Charlie's record and had him figured as a gung-ho buccaneer with more bravery than brains. Wanted to teach him restraint sometimes won battles as much as daring.

"It's a perfect setup," Boyd said.

The lines and angles in Charlie's mind dissolved as he wiped the slate clean to visualize the attack. The supply ship approached along a base course of 195 degrees. Zigged southwest just in time to offer the submarine a near ninety-degree angle on the bow. A beautiful setup.

He'd fire three torpedoes, just to be sure.

He had to be careful not to expose too much of a broadside profile during the attack. The feather the periscope made in the water became more visible. The submarine also became easier to detect by an alert Japanese sonarman.

In the unforgiving attack trainer, such sloppiness typically resulted in a loss. To make it that far and lose would be heartbreaking.

His last time in the trainer, he wanted to do it right.

A thought nagged until it caught him. He met Grayson's eye.

The man's mouth dropped open. "Ah. Yes. We should do another—"

The perfect setup had distracted Charlie from the primary threat, the DDs. They circled the supply ship in a different pattern. He hadn't made enough observations to complete the picture.

"Up scope!" he barked.

He swung the periscope across the escorts while Grayson rattled off bearings. After a few minutes, he repeated the exercise. The ships looked a lot bigger now.

Boyd: "I've got a pattern."

"Target base course?" Charlie said.

"Holding steady. But our perfect setup ain't perfect."

He returned to the plotting table, where Boyd sketched out the destroyers' probable future locations.

Where Charlie hoped to shoot, one of the Asashios would be almost right on top of him. A beautiful way to get detected and rammed. He wiped the sheen of sweat from his upper lip. He could beat himself up later.

"We might shift course and increase speed," Grayson offered. "The target is approaching at one-nine-five. We could come right five, ten degrees."

The idea made sense. The distance to the track would lengthen, but they'd reach the target at a time when the escorts were farther afield.

"Which is it?" Charlie asked the officers. "Five or ten? What's the optimal location to reach the target?"

Boyd rubbed the back of his neck. "I don't know. I don't see it."

Grayson growled, "Let me see. I'll figure it out."

While his officers argued over their meager options, Charlie stepped back from the table and closed his eyes. In his mind, his submarine approached ships moving south by southwest in an elegant pattern.

The way Quiet Bill had set up the escorts to hug the target made Charlie glad the man was on his side. He studied the plot for an opening.

He might get a shot off without detection, but he had

to thread the needle. Each sweep of the destroyers offered little windows of opportunity.

And one big one, he realized, though it presented an even bigger gamble.

"What about a long-range shot?" Grayson asked the men.

Rohm rubbed his jaw. "Maybe. I don't know. Target that small?"

"What are you thinkin', Harrison?" Boyd drawled.

"Keep her so," Charlie said. Maintain her present heading.

Grayson sighed. "You must be joking."

"Nope."

Boyd said, "Didn't you know? Ol' Harrison here don't have a joking bone in his body, Gray."

The men chuckled.

Grayson: "What's the plan?"

"When they're almost on top of us, we go deep," Charlie explained. "After they pass over, we rise to periscope depth and fire three shots up the target's skirt. The one place the DDs aren't guarding is directly behind the Kinesaki."

Rohm nodded. "Then we pull the plug and head out, balls to the wall."

"Right." Charlie glanced at Quiet Bill, whose mouth twitched into a brief smile.

"Your idea isn't terrible," Grayson said. "But our fish have to hit a bulls-eye."

The torpedoes had to fire at the ship's receding stern, a target just thirty feet wide. Grayson was right. Bulls-eye or nothing.

It was also their best shot.

"Come left to three-five-zero," Charlie said. "Time since last look?"

"Six minutes," Rohm told him.

"Up scope. Observation."

Bearing, range, angle on the bow. Rohm turned knobs on the TDC.

The tension built while the approach party worked as a team to execute their plan. Periscope checks to confirm or tune the variables fed into the TDC. Minor course adjustments. Charlie forgot it was just a game. His training took over as he went through the precise and grinding routine that built toward the catharsis of attack.

He looked around the dummy conning tower and imagined it jammed with pipes, valves, and gauges. The diesel oil smell. Monstrous engines pulsing.

"Rig to dive," he said. "Up scope. Final observation."

The model ships crawled across the sea. Very large now.

"Come and get it," he murmured. "Down scope. Dive, dive, dive! Take us down to 200 feet."

"Final depth, 200 feet," Grayson reported.

"Time until next zig?"

"Five minutes."

Charlie nodded. Plenty of time. "Rig for silent running."

"All compartments rigged for silent running. We're in the crucible."

Boyd smirked and shook his head at Grayson's choice of words. Rohm cast an anxious glance at the ceiling. The Japanese ships were now passing overhead. Charlie imagined the churn of propellers, *whoosh whoosh whoosh*. Sweat trickled down his spine and soaked through his service khakis.

"Target is Kinesaki-class supply ship," he said. "We'll fire three torpedoes at his stern from a thousand yards. Aft torpedo, make ready the stern tubes."

"Stern tubes ready!" Rohm said.

"Order of tubes is one, two, three. High speed, depth four feet."

Grayson looked up from his stopwatch. "They're past us, Harrison."

"Very well. Planes, periscope depth."

"Depth, sixty-five feet."

"Up scope." He swiveled the periscope. "All clear. No aircraft." He settled the reticle on his target. "Gotcha."

"What do you see?" Grayson said from the other side of the periscope.

"I'm looking right at his stern. Aft torpedo, stand by. Final bearing, mark!"

"Two-one-zero!"

"Range, mark!"

"Nine hundred yards!"

"Angle on the bow, zero! Speed, twelve knots!"

"Set!" Rohm cried from the TDC. "Shoot anytime!"

"Fire torpedoes!" Charlie ordered.

Rohm pressed the firing plunger. "Firing one! First shot is on the way!" He counted seconds. "Firing two! Firing three!"

"Down scope! Take her down to 300 feet, all ahead full!"

"Torpedoes running hot, straight, and normal." Rohm squinted at Quiet Bill and muttered, "At least, I hope so. Estimate sixty seconds to impact."

As Rohm counted down, Charlie gazed hopefully at his teacher.

Quiet Bill smiled. "Boom."

CHAPTER THREE
JUDGE AND JURY

Japanese resistance on Guadalcanal had ended in February, and American forces swept to New Georgia, continuing an island-hopping strategy they hoped would take them to Japan. Navy pilots bombed a convoy of troop transports at the Battle of the Bismarck Sea in March. P38 fighters shot down a bomber plane carrying Admiral Yamamoto, the architect of the Pearl Harbor attack, in April. American forces recaptured the Aleutian Islands in May.

While Charlie attended PXO School in Connecticut, he'd missed it all.

In Europe, the German Sixth Army surrendered at Stalingrad. The Afrika Korps retreated to Tunisia. The Allies were close to securing North Africa, exposing southern France, Italy, and the Balkans to invasion.

The tide was turning, and Charlie itched to get back in the fight. Which explained his galloping pulse as he made his way to the commander's office.

Lieutenant-Commander Bill Hutchison had requested to see him. This being wartime, boards didn't convene to qualify exec candidates. It was all up to Quiet Bill's judgment. With a word, he could yank Charlie from the boats forever.

Charlie approached the young ensign sitting behind a desk in the reception room. "Lieutenant Charles Harrison, reporting to the commander as ordered."

The ensign smirked at Charlie's hangdog face. He tilted his head toward Quiet Bill's closed door. "You're late, Mr. Harrison. The commander's sore."

Charlie checked his watch. "I thought I was early. It's not yet 1500."

The smirk disappeared. "Ah, I see. So you're the one."

"The one what?"

"Each class, the commander picks one of the guys and gives him the wrong time for a meeting. Then he chews him up and spits him out."

"You're kidding me."

"He transferred one poor bastard off submarines. Tread careful in there."

Charlie shifted his weight and swallowed. "I will. Thanks."

"Digby!" Quiet Bill shouted through his office door. "For Chrissakes, leave Harrison alone and send him in."

"Aye, aye, sir!" The ensign grinned up at Charlie. "The commander will see you now, Mr. Harrison."

Charlie smiled with narrowed eyes, partly to convey, "Nice one, kid." And to add, "I'm committing your name and face to memory."

Even with a war on, the Navy preserved its stalwart hazing tradition.

Quiet Bill occupied a creaking chair behind a big desk stacked with papers. Like everything in the Navy, the desk was drab and built to last forever. A fan startled papers but did little to reduce the oppressive July heat.

Behind him, filing cabinets stood at attention against the wall, each packed with student files. Young men who went on to bright careers in the boats. Unfortunates who washed out and found themselves in for another line of work.

Charlie stood at attention. "Reporting to the commander as ordered, sir."

"Grab a chair, Harrison." He thumbed open a file folder and scanned its contents. "Two war patrols. Ran the gun crew that sank the *Mizukaze* in the Solomon Sea. Got a Silver Star for the action. In the Celebes Sea, you took command and sank *Yosai*. Put some holes in a light carrier and a heavy cruiser, which rammed another cruiser and sank him. Got a boatload of refugees home. Awarded the Navy Cross. An exemplary contribution to the war effort."

"Thank you, sir." So far, so good, though he sensed a "but" coming.

"*Hara-kiri*, they call you. Men like you are showing that some things aren't impossible, only unlikely. Not to mention proving twenty years of doctrine wrong. Some might say you were reckless, though. Reckless and lucky. They think you're an outlier, statistically speaking."

Spoken like a true submariner. Submariners loved their statistics. In undersea combat, nothing was certain. All outcomes were calculated probabilities.

"Big rewards usually have big risks attached," Charlie said.

"Like when you ran off on your own to fight the Japs on Mindanao?"

There it was. The "but."

Charlie's spine tingled. "That was complicated, sir. It seemed like the right call at the time."

The commander scratched a fresh note in his file. "Uh-huh." He slapped the folder shut. "I heard something else. Something not in the file. Some business about modifying your fish. If that's true, you took one hell of a risk. You could have blown up your boat."

Charlie said nothing.

The commander frowned. "All right—"

"I took a lot of risks when I was in command of *Sabertooth*, sir. But every one of them was a calculated risk."

Quiet Bill eyed him a moment longer but dropped it. If Charlie had modified torpedoes but was still serving in the submarines, somebody high up had buried it.

"It's all in the past," the man said. "I'm concerned about the future. I assume you heard the scuttlebutt about Congressman May shooting his mouth off."

"I did, sir."

Everybody at the school knew about it. Chairman of the Committee on Military Affairs Andrew May toured the Pacific Theater and held a press conference when he got home. He told the press not to worry about American submariners because the Japanese set their depth charges too shallow.

Thanks to this valuable intelligence, the IJN would correct its mistake. The enemy had already bagged seventeen submarines so far in the war. A thousand souls rested in the deep. That number might now well skyrocket.

"Back in April, after we blew Admiral Yamamoto out of the sky, the Japs executed three of the Doolittle Tokyo Raiders," the commander went on. "Lined them up and shot them like dogs. Firing squad. Promised a one-way ticket to Hell for any more pilots they captured."

America responded to the Pearl Harbor attack by launching sixteen B25 bombers, normally land-based, from the carrier *Hornet*. The planes bombed Tokyo and other installations but couldn't return. They crash-landed in China. Colonel Doolittle's raid had boosted morale across the home front.

Charlie wasn't sure where the commander was going with all this.

Quiet Bill growled, "The thing is, we're getting cocky, and they're getting desperate. The war isn't going to end anytime soon. It's just going to get nastier and bloodier. We need our best out there in the boats. Understand?"

A trickle of sweat ran down Charlie's back. "Yes, sir."

"You'd be the first exec who hasn't run every department at least once, especially engineering. The first with only two war patrols under his belt. You follow me, son?"

"Yes, sir." This was it. Quiet Bill wasn't going to qualify him.

"Qualification as an exec is similar to qualification for command. Do you think you're ready to command, Harrison?"

No, Charlie thought with brutal honesty. He'd tasted it, though, and he wanted it. "Is anybody really ready?"

For him, it was not a rhetorical question.

Quiet Bill sighed. "As good an answer as one could give, I guess." The man's eyes flickered across Charlie's sweat-greased face. "Relax, Harrison. I'm qualifying you for exec."

Charlie grinned before he could catch himself. "Outstanding, sir."

"Despite the deficiencies in your experience, you've shown yourself to be a mature CO and team player over the last three months. You're cool under fire. It'd be a bigger mistake to take you off the submarines than leave you in." He gazed at Charlie with concern. "You're sweating like a pig. Too hot in here?"

"I was worried," Charlie admitted.

"Qualification doesn't mean you get detailed," Quiet Bill reminded him.

His heart sank. Now comes the bad news. "Of course, sir."

"As it happens, the commanders agreed with my reservations. Nobody would have you." The man raised his hands. "Hang on a second. I'm not finished. Nobody, that is, except one. Gilbert Moreau."

Charlie's eyes widened. He couldn't believe it. "Captain Moreau of the *Sandtiger*?"

"You want the posting? She's just finishing up a refit at Mare Island."

"Are you kidding? The man's a legend!"

"He's one of our best, for sure. As good as Mush Morton. Big risk taker, like you. I hope you all survive the war."

Charlie pushed his chair back and jumped to his feet. "Thank you for everything, sir. When do I leave?"

The commander cocked an eyebrow. "Don't you want to graduate first? Then you can talk to the detailing officer. He'll tell you everything you need to know."

Charlie reminded himself never to show emotion to a superior officer. He forced his expression into one of sullen competence. "Yes. Of course, sir."

The old submariner shook his head. "Chomping at the bit to kill some more Japs." He swiveled in his chair to jam Charlie's file in its proper cabinet. "Captain Moreau

is going to love you, Harrison. Dismissed. Good luck
to you."

CHAPTER FOUR

HOMECOMING

The troop train pounded across America, hauling Sherman tanks and boxcars filled with khaki-clad servicemen. The soldiers played acey-deucey, smoked, sang bawdy songs, read *Batman* and *Tarzan* comic books. As the days grew hotter, they pulled down the windows and lounged in their skivvies. Once a day, they poured from the train for physical training, sometimes a lukewarm shower from the water tanker's spout. At night, they slept in foldout bunks veiled by curtains.

A member of a solitary brotherhood, Charlie kept to himself. He'd served in the submarines long enough he didn't mind being cooped up so long. He sat by the window and gazed out. Big cities, small towns, mountains, and farmland rolled past. Amazing, this country, how big and beautiful and worth fighting for. He celebrated Independence Day watching fireworks bang over Chicago.

Every mile of track brought him closer to his new command. Closer to the city where he grew up. The future and the past. Destiny, his friend Rusty had called it. It was out there waiting for him, but first he had to get there.

Whistle shrieking, the train chugged into the San Francisco station right on schedule. Young Marines roared and waved from the windows. All headed for the Pacific. Charlie had heard them brag about killing Japs, watched them write anxious letters to loved ones. Many wouldn't be coming home, and they knew it.

Charlie scanned the crowd as the train gasped to a halt, exhaling steam. His heart sank. He'd sent a telegram from New London, but she hadn't come.

He shouldered his sea bag and stepped off the train into the crowd.

"Charlie!"

The feminine voice pierced him like a bullet. He spun in place, head bobbing for a better look. Shouting Marines surged around him.

"Over *here!*"

She stood on her tiptoes, waving at the end of the platform.

Charlie grinned and waved back. "Evie!"

He pushed through the swirling khaki crowd until he stood in front of her, still wearing a big dumb grin. She beamed back at him. A simple gray short-sleeved dress sheathed her body.

Evie looked fantastic.

She launched into a hug, squeezing him for all she was worth. "Well, look at you!"

His heart pounded in his ears as he held her warm

body. Her scent brought an avalanche of memories. "God, Evie. It's great to see you."

"You and me both!" She took a step back. "So how long do we have?"

"Only a few hours. I have to report to my new CO."

"Well, that is TB. Too bad." She took his hand. "Come on, then!"

Evie pulled him off the platform and onto the busy, sun-washed sidewalk. Charlie followed with hesitant steps, taking it all in. The city had changed, bustling with war effort. They headed toward the waterfront.

"What have you been doing with yourself?" he asked her.

"Working at the Ford plant. I'm a Rosie the Riveter. Like that song by The Four Vagabonds?" She bent her arm and flexed her bicep. "We can do it!"

"I don't know that song," said Charlie, amused and bewildered.

"The factory doesn't make cars anymore. We finish tanks, mostly. Send them off to the Pacific to fight. Picture me in overalls with a scarf wrapped around my head, holding a rivet gun."

"I'll bet you're a babe even in that outfit," he told her.

She punched his shoulder. "When I'm not doing that, I work on my victory garden, sell war bonds, give blood, hand in my empty toothpaste tubes. Everybody's busy these days. Too bad you don't have time to get up to Tiburon."

His hardworking mother and three older sisters had

raised him after his father died back in 1932, during the hard times of the Depression. Despite the hardships of those years, they'd pulled together and done all right. His upbringing by four women had given him a strong mix of confidence and caution. His family's poverty had taught him to be resourceful and put work first.

Probably best he didn't see Mom. He'd broken her heart when he'd gone off to the Naval Academy. America didn't want war, but Charlie saw it as inevitable and wanted to get ahead of the curve. The peacetime draft came just a few years later.

If he went home, he wasn't sure he'd be able to leave again.

"I have a stack of letters," Charlie said. "Can you deliver them for me?"

"I sure can." Evie paused in front of a tavern and caught her breath. "And here we are. One of the few bars where they serve liquor to our brave fighting men. Buy me a drink, sailor?"

He winced, remembering Jane saying those exact words on a beach in Oahu. He recovered with a smile. "Sure."

They walked onto a veranda overlooking the bay and sat at one of the tables. Most of the patrons wore uniforms. A propaganda poster on the wall warned servicemen against syphilis. Charlie asked for a Schlitz. Evie wanted a Manhattan but ordered a hurricane. Whiskey was in short supply, with most distilleries converted to produce industrial alcohol for torpedo fuel.

America was at war. All of it was. People and industry, body and mind. Total war. Victory or nothing, no matter what it took, no matter how long it lasted.

After their drinks arrived, Evie nattered about home. Her father volunteered as a coastal watcher. The women's dress code raised the hems on dresses to save cloth for the war effort. She bought the dress she was wearing for seven ration coupons, a bargain. Her mother had gotten good at canning garden vegetables.

Charlie didn't say much, just watching her. He enjoyed listening to her talk about home while the beer warmed his chest. She seemed excited to see him, maybe a bit nervous. Her last letter implied the door was open to possibility. By the time he read it, he'd already moved on, though the fire he and Jane had kindled on Oahu had been a dalliance, not much more.

Seeing his Evie again stirred him up. Memories, each loaded with feeling, flooded his mind. Sitting here in her glow, he realized how much he'd missed her. Not the idea but the genuine article. Bright smile, crazy moods, and all. Before he ran off to the Academy, she'd been his best friend as well as his girl.

Charlie sensed an opportunity to get her back. She could be his girl again. He didn't know the words. He had no right to ask her to wait. He had to earn it somehow, but with so little to offer a woman, he didn't know how to do that.

His eyes dropped to her bosom while she talked. He

remembered being with her before he joined the Navy, dozens of intimate moments.

Unbidden, another memory intruded. Him and Jane fumbling in his dark room at the Royal Hawaiian, his hand grazing her soft, pert breast.

His cheeks flushed with heat. God, had he been cheating on Evie? Was he now cheating on Jane? He shifted his gaze to the bay and watched the boats. Wind swept and rippled the water.

"You're thinking about her, aren't you?"

His cheeks burned. "What? Who do you mean?"

"The Navy. No, not the Navy. The war. You went and married it."

She may not have understood him like Jane did, but she had him figured out.

"I don't have a lot to give a woman right now. Nothing real, anyway." There, he said it. He wanted her, sure. But he didn't think he could have her. Taking her back would be unfair.

She sighed. "I wasn't talking about us. I was talking about you. Don't give too much of yourself to this war."

"I'm going to live through this," Charlie assured her. "I promise I will."

"I believe you. One day, peace will come. When it's over, you have to be able to come home. You have to be able to give yourself to another cause."

Charlie thought about Jack Reynolds, the S-55's exec. So consumed by his hatred of the Japanese that, even if he had lived, he wouldn't have survived the war.

"I'm taking the war one day at a time," he said.

"You and your naval gazing," Evie sighed and added, "That was a pun." She looked him dead in the eye and set her empty glass down. "You're going to buy me another one of these, Charlie Harrison, and keep 'em coming."

CHAPTER FIVE

HOME FRONT

Charlie boarded a ferry bound for the Mare Island Naval Shipyard. There, he'd find Captain Moreau and *Sandtiger*, at the base for an overhaul.

He had time to think on the hour-long journey. He'd made the right decision about Evie but still felt a strong longing. Seeing her had inflicted a piercing loneliness. His short visit to San Francisco had only made him homesick.

As the ferry passed Alcatraz, he gazed west beyond the Golden Gate Bridge into the Pacific's blue haze. His return to duty would focus his restless brain. Life was a lot simpler out there, cruising the deep.

Back in San Francisco, the afternoon fog rolled in and shrouded the city. The ferry chugged past Tiburon. Charlie gaped at the landmarks, each bringing up a childhood memory. He blew a kiss to his mom and sisters.

The boat reached Mare Island and warped to the dock. Sailors hoisted their sea bags and tromped down the gangplank. Charlie asked directions. He stowed his bag in his room and went to the officer's club, where he hoped to find Moreau.

Sitting at a corner table with two men, *Sandtiger*'s commander played poker. Buzz cut, bushy eyebrows, big nose, heavy jowls, square shoulders. A bear of a man. A lit cigar protruded from meaty lips. Face flushed with liquor, the captain scowled at him.

"Who could dis be?" he said in a thick Cajun accent. He waved Charlie forward. "Come see, boy."

Charlie stood at attention. "Lieutenant Charles Harrison, sir. Reporting—"

"Well, well!" The captain grinned at the other players. "Dis here boy is my new exec, and just in time too. Fierce one, ain't he?"

One of the men looked up at Charlie. Balding, slim, gray eyes sharp as flint. Lieutenant-commander insignia on his collar. Another submarine captain. "Just in time is right. God, look at him. Just a kid."

"Kid sank the *Mizukaze*, Frank. Avenged the 56."

"Ah," the captain said. "You're that Harrison."

His imperious impression didn't change. Charlie couldn't tell if being *that* Harrison was good or bad in his book.

"Second time out, he sank *Yosai*," Moreau said. "They call him *Hara-kiri*. What'd you do on your last patrol, you sumbitch? Sink some sampans, did ya?"

The captain shook his head. "You always did like the wildcards, Gil."

"He ain't wild. He's an ace of spades. He's my ace

now. Charlie, dis here is Cap'n Rickard, commands the *Redhorse*. Cap'n Shelby, the *Warmouth*. Fighting captains. The best of the best."

Shelby leaned back in his chair. His frank, friendly face broke into a crooked smile. "God help you with this maniac, Harrison."

"We're gonna kill us some Japs." Moreau bared his teeth and rubbed his big paws together. "A whole lot of 'em. Big mission ComSubPac is cookin' up for us maniacs. Real big." He squinted through a puff of cigar smoke. "Sail tomorrow, Charlie boy. Tonight, you got liberty."

Caught flatfooted, Charlie didn't say a word. *Sandtiger* wasn't scheduled to go to sea for another week. He'd hoped to help prepare the boat for sea and learn her systems, particularly her new upgrades. Maybe stay aboard the submarine the whole time and get used to coping with his claustrophobia.

Thrown into the pool again. Sink or swim, and he'd better swim.

"You're from here, ain't you?" the captain asked him. "Go home. See your mama. Kiss your girlfriend. May be the last time you do it. Be back tomorrow bright and early. Now go on, sunshine. Git."

Charlie left the captains hunched over their poker game.

"Harrison!"

Two young officers waved from a nearby table. The man on the left slouched in wrinkled service khakis with a smirk etched on his bland face. His clean-cut comrade sat ramrod straight, blinking nervously. Empty beer bottles littered the table next to an overflowing ashtray.

The slouch offered his hand. "Gerald Percy, communications. This is Tom Nixon, engineering."

Charlie shook it. "Nice to meet you fellas."

Percy didn't let go. "Help me up. We're getting out of here."

He hauled the officer to his feet. The man staggered against him.

"You all right?" Charlie asked.

"Better than all right, Exec. I'm deep in the sauce."

Charlie shot a curious look at Nixon, who stood smiling shyly with his hands fidgeting in his pockets. "What about him?"

"He doesn't drink. He's plain certifiable, though."

"Where are you fellas off to?"

"San Francisco. Got to pick up some stuff before we take off tomorrow. Stuff the boat needs. Want to tag along?"

Charlie pictured the rest of the night lying on his bunk. "Sure." Being around people instead would be good for him. "Count me in."

He feared Percy would be a chatterbox during the ferry ride, but Nixon did most of the talking while the communications officer leaned on the gunwale and smirked at the view. The engineering officer opened up once Charlie brought up the refit.

"They mounted a new deck gun—a five-inch pulled off an S-boat—on the forward deck," Nixon told him. "Replaced the twenty-millimeter ack-acks with forty-millimeter Bofors. Installed ammo stowage on deck for the machine guns—"

"Tell him about the bridge," Percy said.

"The sheltered bridge is *gone*. They cut it down. Took out the surface steering and the plating on the periscope shears. The smaller silhouette makes the boat harder to see. We have new SJ radar too, more reliable and able to detect ships at a longer range. PPI added to the radar. New engines, motors, wiring. More limber holes in the hull to let out trapped air, so we can dive faster."

Percy lit a cigarette with a steel lighter. "Don't forget the bathythermograph."

Nixon nodded like a priest asked a question about God. "Oh, I was getting to *that*. You know the ocean is made of thermal layers. Water temperature varies according to how deep it is. These thermal layers affect sonar; they reflect and scatter sonar pings. *Sandtiger* now has its very own bathythermograph, which records the temperature of the water around the boat and puts that info right in the conning tower. Allows us to hide from the Japs."

Charlie agreed it was an amazing innovation.

Percy snorted. "If it works."

Nixon shrugged. "Well, yeah. What you said."

Sandtiger sounded loaded. Charlie couldn't wait to take her out.

Percy pointed. "There she is. You can just see her behind *Warmouth.*"

Charlie caught a glimpse of the gray submarine's nose. The salty bay breeze brought a whiff of diesel oil stench. He breathed deep.

Almost home, he thought.

God, Evie was right about him.

Percy's objective turned out to be Pirate's Cove, another of the city's few establishments allowed to serve liquor to men in uniform. Sailors and soldiers filled the place. Percy found them space at the bar. The bartender welcomed him by name and plonked three cold bottles of beer on the counter. He next lined up three shots and filled them to the brim.

The communications officer raised his shot glass. "Welcome to *Sandtiger*, Harrison. Down the hatch."

"Thanks," Charlie said while Percy gulped his liquor. He threw back his own shot and braced as the burning liquid poured down his throat. Splice the mainbrace. Outside, the day was ending. The city would black out soon. He wondered how they were going to get back. "Where's the torpedo officer tonight?"

Percy had already chugged his beer. He scooped up Nixon's shot and tossed it back with a wince. "Hiding in his room, probably. The captain has it in for him."

"What did he do?"

42

"Got on the captain's radar. The captain already kicked our last exec off the boat. Poor Trombly was next on his shit list."

Nixon smirked. "You'll be our third exec in three patrols."

"Bottoms up, sailor," Percy said and took a long pull on Nixon's beer.

Charlie sipped. "What did he do? The exec?"

"The Old Man has anger issues."

Nixon said, "He's a fighter. He pushes the boat hard. Anything goes wrong, anybody can't keep up, the captain doesn't like it."

Percy said, "Shit rolls downhill. The Old Man flushes execs like turds."

Charlie drank the rest of his beer in two long swallows. If these men were being straight with him, his plum assignment might turn out to be his last time out in the submarines. He'd have to tread carefully with Moreau and avoid any mistakes.

After two more rounds, they went back out into the cool night air. The walk helped clear Charlie's buzzing head.

"Aren't we supposed to be getting something for the boat?" he asked.

"Oh, right," the communications officer said. "No, I made that up."

"How are we getting back to the base?"

"The ferries stopped running for the night. We'll catch

the first tomorrow morning." Percy caught Charlie's expression and laughed. "Live a little, Harrison. The way the captain fights, this might be our last time out. And here we are."

Rowdy groups of servicemen trickled in and out of the building. Pounding drums vibrated through the walls.

Charlie followed him to the door. "What is this place?"

"I hope you like to dance, Harrison."

They went in. A swing band roared on the stage. Drums rattled as scores of dancers jitterbugged on the crowded dance floor. Soldiers and sailors twirled smiling women in short dresses. A member of the band stepped out in front for his solo and blew piercing notes on his trumpet.

"Come on," Percy shouted over the music. "The nickel-hoppers are waiting."

Charlie followed him to a booth. Percy told him to buy nine tickets, which cost him a cool ninety cents. He passed them out.

Nixon accepted his with a lopsided smile. "Oh, goodie."

He ran off and gave the ticket to a redhead twice his size. She demurely lifted the hem of her dress and slipped it into her stocking. Nixon grabbed her hand and dragged the big woman onto the dance floor.

"Taxi dancers," Percy said. "Ten cents a dance. The girl gets a nickel."

"Wow. Nixon's a good dancer."

"Yeah. He can really swing. Otherwise, he can barely

look a girl in the eye, much less talk to her. A genius with anything mechanical, though, I'll give him that. Now go out there and cut a rug, champ. If you don't know how to dance, one of the girls will show you the ropes."

Percy staggered toward the women and offered a buxom blonde his ticket with a courtly bow. The woman cut him down with a glance and took his hand. His head heavy and buzzed again, Charlie watched them dance.

Brass gleamed onstage. The band played as if possessed. Horns blared across the bouncing room. Charlie leaned against the wall and tapped his feet. He fingered the tickets in his pocket and thought about dancing.

It all had a frantic quality, a last hurrah before shipping out to the war. For one last night, they reveled and thumbed their noses at death.

His last night too. He was shipping out tomorrow. Percy was right. This could be his last patrol, one way or the other. He should live it up a little. Why not?

Still, Charlie suspected dancing with total strangers would only make him lonelier. Make him miss Evie and Jane even more.

After a few songs, the communications officer stumbled from the press. "Wow, that broad can sure drag a hoof."

"What's the mission?"

Percy regarded him blearily. "What are you talking about?"

"The captain said ComSubPac gave us operations orders that promised some good hunting. I'm curious where we're going."

The man laughed. "Why are you talking about work? For Christ's sake, you're at the Barbary Coast. Go out there and dance. Some of these girls are khaki wacky. A good-looking, earnest guy like you might even get lucky."

"Look, I just got here, and—"

"That does it. I'll find you one who's suitably patriotic." Percy scanned the crowd. "Wow, there's a hot patootie for you. Check out that babe."

Charlie stiffened. Percy was pointing right at Evie.

Evie, laughing while she danced in the arms of a khaki-clad man.

He waded into the crowd.

"That's the spirit, Exec!" Percy called after him.

Charlie grabbed her arm. "Evie! What are you doing here?"

She stared back at him, her mouth an *O*. "What are *you* doing here?"

He had no good answer. He had no good reason to interrupt her dance, either. A large hand landed on his shoulder and squeezed.

"You her boyfriend, pal?" the man growled. He was a Marine.

Evie lifted her chin and appraised Charlie. "No. Apparently, he's not."

The Marine said, "Then you've got three seconds to get the fuck out of here before I come after you. One."

"Sorry I barged in like that, but—"

"Not nearly sorry yet. Two."

"Hey, don't start trouble. If we get caught, it'll go bad for you. I'm an officer."

The man grinned. "So am I."

His fist blurred toward Charlie's face.

Charlie saw it coming. He lunged backward. His back connected with another dancer whose motion shoved him straight into bare knuckles.

The lights went out.

He came to shaking his head as Percy yelled, "Hey, jarhead!" and sucker-punched the Marine in the ear. The man flinched and roared.

Evie: *What the hell is going on?*

"Working Navy here!" Percy yelled.

Marines released their partners and surged toward the scene with clenched fists. A sailor grabbed one by the shoulder, spun him around, and decked him. Women screamed and fled the dance floor as the song abruptly died.

Percy howled and threw himself at the Marines. The trumpet player struck up, "You're a Grand Old Flag," while sailors and Marines laid into each other and Army didn't know whose side to take.

Evie cupped Charlie's face in her hands. "You all right?"

Those who weren't fighting sang, "You're a grand old flag, though you're torn to rag, and forever in peace may you wave!"

Evie's Marine pummeled Percy in a headlock while the buxom blonde pounded the jarhead's back with her fists.

Charlie straightened his shoulders. "Never better."

"Don't do it, Charlie Harrison," she warned. "Don't even think about—"

He kissed her on the mouth. "Sorry about everything, Evie." He sighed as his eyes swept the brawl. "Goddamn honor."

Then he waded into the fight, lashing out with his fists.

The rest of the band joined in to play the song as men roared, *"You're the emblem of the land I love, the home of the free and the brave!"*

Charlie grew up in Tiburon and had often ventured into San Francisco's mean streets looking for work during the Depression. He knew how to fight.

He punched a man in the jaw and doubled over as a fist slammed into his gut. He launched shoulder first against his assailant, knocking him on his ass. Somebody grabbed him from behind. He stomped the man's foot and broke free.

He spun with his fist raised to strike—

"Heat!" a woman screamed.

Whistles blew. Policemen rushed into the Barbary Coast swinging billy clubs while the patrons stampeded for the exits.

Evie grabbed Charlie's hand and pulled. "Come on, you big stupid idiot!"

The band serenaded them on their way out the door with, "Anchors Aweigh."

Percy and the blonde hit the sidewalk laughing and kept going. Charlie and Evie chased after them, navigating by moonlight alone.

"Wait!" Charlie said. "Where's Nixon?"

"Right here," Nixon said from behind. He held the redhead's hand. "I actually punched a man in the face!"

Percy stopped and bent over to catch his breath. "Jesus, Exec. You can fight."

"You men are all idiots," Evie said.

"Taking on that Marine. No wonder they call you 'Hara-kiri.'"

"Evie's right," Charlie said. "I'm a big stupid idiot."

The communications officer smiled. "Hey, we're only getting started."

"What now? We can't head back to base until tomorrow morning."

"Says you. We're going to find us a boat and go back to Mare Island. Show the girls the attack trainer we have set up out there."

The blonde looked confused. "Or we could all just go to my place."

Percy draped his arm over her shoulders. "You'll love the attack trainer, Betty darling. I'll bet any man alive you sink a Jap ship on your first go."

Betty shrugged. "Sure. Why not?"

"You all go ahead," Charlie said. "I'm going to stick around. I'll catch the first ferry out to the island."

The foursome walked off into the darkness, singing, "You're a Grand Old Flag."

"My crew," Charlie told Evie.

She socked his shoulder hard. "What were you doing at the Barbary Coast when you told me you had to report to your CO, whatever that is?!"

"I did." He yelped as she hit him again. "Honest! The captain told me I had the night off. I ran into Percy and Nixon, and they brought me here. That's it."

"I didn't see you on the dance floor," she said.

"Because I wasn't. To be honest, I was missing you. Your turn."

"I have to explain? There's a war on, Charlie. The government rations almost everything, and what isn't costs a lot of money, more than I can afford on my salary at the plant. I make good side money at the dance hall. I come down twice a week. Don't you dare tell my mom and dad about it, or I'll kill you."

"I won't."

Her explanation sobered him. While everybody back home lived on strict rationing for the war effort, submariners ate fresh meat and eggs. They were the best-fed branch of the service.

"I also get lonely," she said. "To be completely honest. I can't have you, but I haven't met anybody yet who can replace you. I just want a little contact."

Charlie understood that too, all too well. "I get it, Evie."

Her eyes gleamed in the moonlight. She'd always been able to nail him to the wall with those eyes.

He showed her his three dance hall tickets, lifted the hem of her dress a few inches, and slipped them into her stocking.

"Guess I'm yours for the next ten minutes," she said. "Where to?"

They entered an all-night movie theater and found a remote spot to sit. Around them, snoring servicemen slept off their benders. On the silver screen, Spencer Tracy told Katharine Hepburn she didn't spend enough time with him.

Evie snorted. She took his hand and squeezed. "How's your face?"

Charlie touched his sore cheekbone and sighed. "I'll have a shiner tomorrow. My CO's going to love that."

"TB, Charlie Harrison. So what's she like?"

"What's who like?"

Her voice dropped to a whisper. "The war."

What was it like?

The submarine gliding through the depths, each creak of the hull reminding him how badly the ocean wanted inside. Depth charges pounding the boat. Japanese sailors screaming in a burning oil slick.

So much tedium. Fear. Misery. Horror.

But also elation.

51

There was nothing like it, combat. The rush of it. Endless tension, sudden catharsis. He never felt so alive. As much as he feared it, he wanted to face it again. He wanted to face himself again as he really was.

No way could Evie ever understand that. He didn't *want* her to understand it.

"She's the devil I know," he said. A devil he'd made a deal with.

Evie said nothing. He thought about kissing her again.

On the big screen, Fay Bainter said, "Success is no fun unless you share it with someone."

Evie nestled against his shoulder, the one she favored punching. "I still love you, Charlie Harrison."

"I ..."

"Oh, shut it. Go back to your war. But come home to me, okay? Promise."

"I promise," Charlie said. "I'll come home. I'll come home to you."

She let out an explosive yawn. "Good."

Tracy told Hepburn to go to the gala without him.

Charlie said, "I love you too, you know."

She began to snore.

CHAPTER SIX

ARTICLES OF WAR

At dawn, he jogged toward the docks on three hours of sleep. Charlie stretched out on the ferry's deck and napped the whole way back to Mare Island.

He showered and shaved in the barracks. Knocked back a quick breakfast in the mess hall. Then he hurried to the wharf where *Sandtiger* lay moored between *Redhorse* and *Warmouth*.

Charlie had spent his first three years in the Navy among large surface ships. When he reported to the S-55, her size had struck him. A game little fighter, but tired, outclassed. *Sandtiger* exuded confidence.

Built by the Electric Boat Company, the *Gato*-class submarine was 311 feet long and twenty-seven feet wide at the beam. Six forward tubes, four aft with a complement of twenty-four torpedoes. Four diesel engines drove her at a top speed of twenty knots on the surface, four electric motors at up to nine knots while submerged. She could dive to 300 feet and range 11,000 miles or seventy-five days. While surfaced, she displaced more than 1,500 tons of water.

The Navy yard had completely repaired and refitted her. Instantly visible was the streamlined superstructure, which enabled her to sail with a lower silhouette.

With her new upgrades, *Sandtiger* was one of the deadliest war machines ever built for sea. True, she was no match for destroyers designed to hunt and kill submarines. Her neutral buoyancy promised a swift sinking if shot or ramming holed her. She had surprise on her side, however. She could travel deep into enemy territory, deliver a sudden and vicious attack.

The submarine's horizontal surfaces were black, her vertical surfaces gray. Even with a fresh paint job, *Sandtiger*'s visible scars made her look like a junkyard dog mauled by too many fights. She'd given far worse than she'd taken, though. Ten sinkings in the last three patrols alone. More than 30,000 tons of Japanese steel and engineering sent to the bottom.

The proud submarine's battle flag waved on the clothesline stretching from the bow to the periscope supports. It displayed a grinning shark wearing a sailor's hat. That and ten patches, one for each enemy ship sunk in combat. Beneath, the Jolly Roger fluttered in the breeze. *Sandtiger* was a buccaneering ship.

Dungareed pirates swarmed the deck, making her ready for sea. Trucks pumped water and diesel into the tanks. Shirtless men hauled boxes of food down the hatch like a train of worker ants. A crane lowered a torpedo into the forward weapons hatch. Charlie hurried across the gangplank with his sea bag.

Percy tossed him a lazy wave. "Welcome aboard, Harrison." He called out to a passing sailor, "Hey, Shorty! Stow the exec's bag."

Charlie looked around. "Tell me we're on schedule."

"You'll be able to take her out on time."

He checked in with the quartermaster and the chiefs, who had the loading well in hand. The men knew what they were doing. He hustled from one spot to the next, listening and learning more than leading. Within several hours, the last of the ship's stores went down the hatch.

Percy whistled to get his attention. "Look lively. Captain's coming."

Captain Moreau ambled along the pier with his hands in his pockets. He took in every detail of the submarine with a single glance. Seemingly satisfied, he came aboard.

Charlie presented himself and saluted. "Welcome aboard, Captain. The loadout is complete. All hands present. Shore power and phone cabling are disconnected."

Moreau gave him a quick once-over. "I hope you gave more than you got."

"Yes, sir," Charlie said.

"Have the men fall in at quarters."

Charlie bawled out the order. The crew mustered on deck abaft of the bridge. They stood at parade rest in the warm afternoon air, fifty-four enlisted men plus the officers. On *Sandtiger*'s port side, *Warmouth* fired its engines, belching smoke from the exhaust vents. The submarine blasted its foghorn as it backed away from the pier. The crew returned waves to the crowd of well-wishers while a Navy band sent them off.

The captain inspected Percy's brash face. The communications officer smirked back at him with a busted lip.

"How'd your gal do?"

"She sank a freighter, Captain. I think I'm in love."

"She do dat to your face after, or were you in the exec's dust-up?"

"I had the exec's back, Skipper."

"All right, Jerry. As long as you saved some for the Japs."

The captain continued his inspection. He paused in front of Nixon. The engineering officer offered him a nervous smile.

"Uh-huh," Moreau muttered. "This guy."

Then he stopped again in front of the next officer, who stood with his sea bag resting on the deck next to him.

Charlie caught his breath. Jack Liebold stared back at him with wide, watery eyes. Charlie and Liebold had served together on *Sabertooth*.

The captain chuckled. "Won him in a poker game last night." He mounted to the bridge, Charlie following. "We lost twenty hands to new construction, replaced with greenhorns. They're yours. Teach their hands to war."

"Aye, Captain."

Moreau handed him a book. "Time to start their education. Read it out loud to the men."

He glanced at the cover. The Articles for the Government of the U.S. Navy. He cracked it open and read, "'The Navy of the United States shall be governed by the following articles. Article 1. The commanders of all fleets, squadrons, naval stations, and vessels belonging to the Navy are required to show in themselves a good example of virtue, honor, patriotism, and subordination.'"

"Skip ahead to Article 4. Just the underlined parts."

"Aye, aye." He flipped the page and belted out, "'Article 4! The punishment of death…may be inflicted upon any person who…in time of battle, displays cowardice, negligence, or disaffection, or withdraws from or keeps out of danger to which he should expose himself…or does not, upon signal for battle, use his utmost exertions to join in battle…or does not do his utmost to overtake and capture or destroy any vessel which it is his duty to encounter.'"

On *Sandtiger*'s starboard side, *Redhorse* backed from the pier, puffing clouds of white smoke like a giant cigar. Its foghorn blared.

Moreau said, "That's enough for now."

The crew stood at respectful attention. They were afraid of the enemy. The captain wanted them to be terrified of him.

Charlie dismissed the men, who rushed to stations. The engines rumbled to life. "Stand by to single up! Take in the gangway!" He roared the commands even as his mind scrambled over the checklist needed to get the boat underway. He was XO now. Everything he did and said needed to convey total confidence.

Charlie turned to the captain. "Engines have full loading. We're ready to get underway, sir."

"Very well. Take us out on time."

"Single up! Take in two and three! Take in four! Take the strain on one!" The lines slithered onto the deck. "Take in one!"

The foghorn blasted. Potential energy surged through the boat as the diesels pulsed. Charlie's chest hummed as *Sandtiger*'s power flowed through him.

Percy blew a whistle, which signaled the sailors to lower and remove the colors. Charlie backed *Sandtiger* into the bay, underway at last.

"Helm, all ahead two-thirds," he ordered with a fierce and sudden joy. "Right twenty degrees rudder."

"Aye, aye, Exec," came the reply over the bridge intercom.

The great fleet submarine churned the water in pursuit of *Redhorse*, which steamed down Mare Island Strait. Well-wishers waved final goodbyes from the pier as the band's rendition of "Anchors Aweigh" faded.

Percy waved in the direction at the departing submarines. "Bye, Trombly!"

One of the lookouts let out a wolf-whistle. A solitary figure ran along the pier, shouting across the distance.

Charlie smiled as he recognized Evie dressed in her gray factory overalls. She stopped at the edge and stood on tiptoes, waving her scarf over her head.

He'd been right. Even in grimy overalls, she was a looker.

"Isn't that your girl, Harrison?" Percy asked him. "I mean, sort of your girl?"

"She is," he replied. "Sort of."

"Well, go on, boy," Moreau said. "You know what to do."

Charlie waved back until she shrank from view. *Sandtiger* rounded Mare Island and entered San Pablo Bay.

The captain said, "Now put her out of your mind. We got work to do."

Charlie's expression flipped back to professional sullen. "Aye, Captain."

"I got an exec who lusts for yellow blood and a torpedo officer who can do the same hoodoo to my fish he did to *Sabertooth*'s. Can't wait to sink some Japs."

He was starting to like Captain Moreau. "Any word on the mission, sir? Last night, you said ComSubPac had something big planned for us."

"He surely does, Charlie. *Redhorse*, *Warmouth*, and us, we're gonna be a wolf pack. We're gonna tear Tojo a new asshole."

CHAPTER SEVEN

THE MISSION

Landfall.

Oahu, pretty as a postcard.

Standing on the bridge, Charlie scanned ahead with his binoculars.

Warmouth and *Redhorse* trailed smoke at the front of the column. The PC boat arrived on time, flashing recognition signals. Paced by this escort, the wolf pack steamed along the bright coastline. To starboard, Honolulu sprawled under lush tropical mountains.

The Royal Hawaiian Hotel. Waikiki Beach. Tiny figures splashed in the surf. Others lounged on the white sand. No doubt, many were submariners on R&R.

Buy me a drink, sailor?

A moment of discomfort. Then he smiled as many more memories flooded his mind's eye. He wondered what Jane was doing right now. He knew she'd returned to duty. Not to the front lines, he hoped. Knowing Jane, though, that's exactly where she'd want to be.

He remembered holding her after she'd woken up crying. Jane had survived the Japanese occupation of the

Philippines. She had her own bad memories, her own nightmares. Still, she wouldn't quit fighting. That just wasn't her.

Percy raised the colors. *Sandtiger*'s proud battle flags streamed in the wind.

Sleek gray destroyers guarded the channel, winding their figure eights. Charlie maneuvered the submarine toward the entrance buoys. A minesweeper chugged past. Planes hummed like hornets overhead, looking for something to sting.

"Permission to bring her into the harbor, Captain?"

Moreau leaned on the gunwale. "Yup."

During the past week at sea, Moreau delegated almost everything to him. Managing the departments, navigation, acting as diving officer during the morning trim dive. A crash course in running a submarine far more rigorous than the firehose treatment Reynolds and Lewis had given him. No screw-ups so far, thank God.

He needed to learn everything he could and make sure the crew learned with him. In accordance with the finest Navy traditions, Charlie gave the firehose treatment to the new ensigns. The chiefs did the same to the enlisted greenhorns in their charge. Charlie relentlessly drilled them all: battle surface, crash dive, fire drill, submerged approach, silent running. By the time *Sandtiger* reached Hawaii, the boat operated at peak efficiency.

The captain seemed satisfied. Otherwise, the skipper remained a bit of a mystery, moody and unpredictable.

Not difficult, though. Certainly not the tyrant Percy had warned him about.

"Helm, Bridge," Charlie said. "Right fifteen degrees rudder. All ahead standard."

The rudder dug into the water and turned the boat into the Pearl Harbor Channel. The water calmed until *Sandtiger* glided across blue glass, like one of Quiet Bill's models.

As always, Pearl buzzed with activity. Dozens of warships lay moored at their berths. Big cranes loomed over the Navy yard, where workers labored to refit a battle-scarred heavy cruiser and two destroyers in dry dock.

Oklahoma still lay where she sank. The shattered listing hulk rested on the harbor bottom. Beyond, *Arizona*'s funnel protruded above the water. Heartbreaking, seeing them again. Charlie had grown up with these battleships and regarded them as giants of the sea. As a teenager, buying and trading, he'd amassed a collection of Topps Gum U.S. Navy cards. Now the giants were dead, and Charlie had become a giant killer.

He piloted the boat across the harbor toward its designated berth at the submarine base, next to a big sea tender. Fuel, water, supply trucks, and a jeep sat on the jetty. The crew warped the boat to the pier and laid the gangplank. Sailors on the dock unloaded mailbags and crates of fresh ice cream and vegetables.

A group of Navy officers dismounted from the jeep

and made their way up the pier to the gangplank. At the sight of the "scrambled eggs" on a peaked cap, Charlie and Percy came to attention and saluted.

"At ease," the man said as he came aboard. He extended his hand to Moreau, who enveloped it in one of his big paws. "Good to see you back in action, Gil."

"It's what I do best, sir."

"Rickard and Shelby are already on their way to the mission briefing."

"Good enough." Moreau jerked his thumb toward Charlie. "Meet my new number two, Charlie Harrison. Eats Japs for breakfast. Charlie, meet the boss, Captain Squadron Commander Rich Cooper."

"An honor to meet you, sir," Charlie said.

"Harrison. Right. ComSubPac mentioned you. *Yosai.* Hell of a thing."

Rear Admiral English had died in a plane crash in February. Rear Admiral Lockwood, who commanded the submarines in the Southwest Pacific, became ComSubPac afterward and transferred his offices to Pearl. Charlie had the honor to meet the man twice. Lockwood, in turn, had taken an interest in him.

Cooper regarded Charlie with a quizzical expression. The squadron commander was a veteran submariner, trained according to pre-war doctrine. Because of that doctrine, the submarines had done little damage so far in the war. Lockwood had begun weeding out complacent captains and replacing them with a new breed of young, aggressive skippers.

The new fighting captains such as Moreau, Rickard, and Shelby were racking up big wins. The results spoke for themselves. Still, veterans like Cooper probably wondered if men like Moreau and Charlie were right in the head.

Maybe like Charlie's old friend Rusty, Cooper defined a hero as a hothead who hadn't yet learned about his mortality. A hothead who got lucky but whose luck would one day run out in accordance with the laws of probability.

Cooper gestured toward one of his officers. "This is Sam Dougherty, E&R officer." Engineering and repair. "He'll make sure your tanks are topped up and help you out with anything else you need. You three boats have top priority. These other men here are inspectors."

As XO, Charlie reviewed readiness reports from department heads. He had a list of repairs ready to give Dougherty.

"Hand over your weep list, and let Nixon run with it, Charlie," Moreau said. "You're coming with me to the mission briefing."

Percy took over as officer of the deck watch. The captain and Charlie climbed into the back of the jeep, which sped off across the jetty. Drab buildings flashed by, headquarters, maintenance, and barracks among groves of waving palm trees.

"The Marines are slogging it out on New Georgia,"

Cooper said over his shoulder. "ComSubPac wants us to do our part and step up our game. Take the fight right to them."

"Dat's why we're here," Moreau said.

"He's cooked up an operation that's right up your alley, Gil."

The jeep braked in front of a headquarters building, a drab boxy structure with flags waving out front.

"Hang tight," Cooper told the driver. "I'll have these men on their way back to their boat in an hour or two."

Inside, the lobby branched off into offices, a typing pool filled with young women, and a large conference room. Rickard and Shelby were already in the conference room with their execs, helping themselves to coffee and doughnuts. Cooper led Moreau and Charlie into the room with the other commanding officers of the wolf pack.

"Now we can start," Shelby said with his crooked grin. "The maniacs are all here. So what's the word?"

Charlie exchanged a curt nod with the other execs and sat at the table. Moreau went to a nearby urn and filled a mug with coffee. One of the admiral's aides passed out thick packets marked TOP SECRET to the captains. These envelopes contained their operations orders from ComSubPac.

OPERATION PAYBACK, Charlie read on its face.

"Gentlemen, welcome," Cooper said. "Today, we're going to launch one of the boldest missions the submarine force has ever undertaken. Your task force is going where no American submarine has gone before."

The men perked up.

"Your destination." Cooper pulled down a giant map of the Pacific Theater over the wall. He swatted a stretch of blue with his pointer. "Area One."

Charlie stifled a gasp. He sat up straight in his chair.

The wolf pack was bound for the Sea of Japan.

CHAPTER EIGHT

HIROHITO'S BATHTUB

The Sea of Japan. Cooper paused to let that sink in.

Surrounded by the Japanese islands to the east and mainland Asia and the Korean peninsula to the west, the Sea of Japan comprised more than 350,000 square miles of open water.

The submariners called it the emperor's private lake. Hirohito's bathtub.

With five straits leading in and out, it was easily defendable. Ships could safely transport troops and war materiel to China and return with food and raw materials. Planes, coastal batteries, ships, and sea mines made it impossible to penetrate.

Until now.

Shelby broke the silence. "What's the mission, exactly?"

"Sink Japanese shipping and go on starving the beast," Cooper said. "We're going to open another front, hit them where they live, and tie up IJN attention and resources." IJN, the Imperial Japanese Navy. "By deploying a coordinated attack group, we'll hit them hard. Send a message. Show the Japs that nowhere is safe. Nowhere on Earth, not even their own backyard."

"They'll be all over us the minute we sink a ship," Rickard said.

"It's the Doolittle Raid all over again," Shelby wondered.

"This is a lightning raid," Cooper clarified. "Sink everything you can in four days. Then get out before the Japs mobilize their defenses. You'll have to make every hour count."

Shelby whistled. "No kidding."

Rickard: "Any intel on how much shipping is running through Area One?"

"None, unfortunately," Cooper said. "Most of their merchant fleet appears to be allocated to the Pacific, running in and out of the big industrial cities on Honshu's eastern coast. However, it stands to reason the western ports are used to ferry reinforcements into the fighting in China. Receive food and raw materials coming the other way. Your attack group will string north to south across likely shipping routes. You should see good hunting."

"Sold," Moreau said. "How the hell do we get in there?"

"Five straits lead into the sea." Cooper tapped the map. "Tartary and La Pérouse in the north, Tsugaru here, and Shimonoseki and Tsushima in the south. PT boats, planes, and ASW mines guard them all. Tsushima, we know, is heavily mined. The Tartar Strait is Russian territory. They've got DDs patrolling it at all times."

Moreau: "So which one gets the prize?"

Another tap. "La Pérouse."

The strait served as a waterway between the islands of Sakhalin and Hokkaido. It separated the Sea of Okhotsk from the Sea of Japan. Cooper said the strait was twenty-five miles long and twenty-seven miles wide at its narrowest part. Between seventy and 130 feet deep, the water rushed in a strong current.

Across its length, the Japanese had planted dense minefields at depths from forty to seventy feet. Others were placed shallower as a threat to surface ships.

A deathtrap for submarines.

Anchored to the sea bottom using steel cables, the mines packed up to 2,500 pounds of explosive. Horns studded the metal spheres. Each horn contained a glass vial filled with acid. Upon contact with a ship's hull, the vial shattered, freeing the acid into a battery. The energized battery detonated the explosive and tore the ship open.

"Commander Voge, ComSubPac's intelligence officer, found us a way through the minefields," Cooper said. "The Japs designed a channel free of surface mines, which allows both its ships and neutral Soviet ships to pass through. All the lend-lease material we send the Russians goes through that strait."

The average draft of Japanese ships was thirty-five feet. Surface ships could travel safely along this safe channel. Submerged submarines couldn't.

"That's our opening," the squadron commander added. "Based on our intel, we have a rough idea of the route the channel takes. As a fallback, at night, the Russians switch on their running lights, which identifies the ship as being with a neutral power."

The Japanese defeated the Russians in 1905. In 1931, Japan invaded Manchuria. As a result, Japan gained control of southern Sakhalin Island, Manchuria, and Korea. After several bloody clashes along the Manchurian-Mongolian border in 1938 and '39, the Soviet Union and the Empire of Japan signed a neutrality pact. This allowed the Soviets to focus on their fight with Germany, the Japanese on their expansion into Asia and the Pacific.

Shelby chuckled. "We're going to follow a Russian ship in there. On the surface. At night."

"Sold," Moreau repeated.

"Do the Russians know about this?" Shelby asked.

"They do not," Cooper said. "Otherwise, I can't describe how we get our intel."

"Roger that."

"This will be a coordinated operation. Frank, you're the senior officer. You'll act as commander of the attack group."

"Very well," Rickard said.

"Rickard's Raiders!" Shelby suggested.

Redhorse's captain shrugged. He didn't care what they

called themselves.

"Better off doing our own thing," Moreau growled. "We don't need a leader. No offense, Frank."

Rickard, amused: "None taken, Gil."

Cooper sighed. "This is the way it's going to be. Remember, you only have four days. You'll have to coordinate your attacks to make the most of it."

"Plenty of meat for everybody," Shelby said.

"Fine," Moreau grunted. "When do we go?"

"Three days," Cooper said. "By then, you'll be provisioned and have any repairs you need completed."

"I understand how we're getting in," Shelby said. "How are we getting out?"

"Same way you got in. We'll create a diversion at one of the Kurile Islands here." The Kuriles were a volcanic archipelago of more than fifty islands that separated the Sea of Okhotsk from the Pacific. "By August 27, *Dartfish* will be on station off Matsuwa. At 0100, he'll start shelling the Jap airfield. Be ready to exit the Japan Sea at that time."

Moreau leaned to his side and murmured, "What you think, boy?"

Charlie considered his answer. Lockwood had rolled the dice on something big. Big rewards and even bigger risks. The rewards were speculative. The risks were known, and they were enormous.

The entry through shallow waters bristling with mines. How little they knew about the territory. The limited time they'd have to sink any ships.

And if the wolf pack got lucky and sank some ships, the Japanese would mobilize everything they had. Sweep the water with radar and planes. Block the exits and starve the submarines out.

Charlie had learned to keep his opinions to himself around a superior officer unless asked a direct question. When asked, he always answered honestly.

"It's a one-way trip," he said.

The captain's face broke into a broad grin. "Probably."

Moreau was right about one thing. He, Rickard, and Shelby were maniacs.

AREA OF OPERATIONS: THE SEA OF JAPAN.

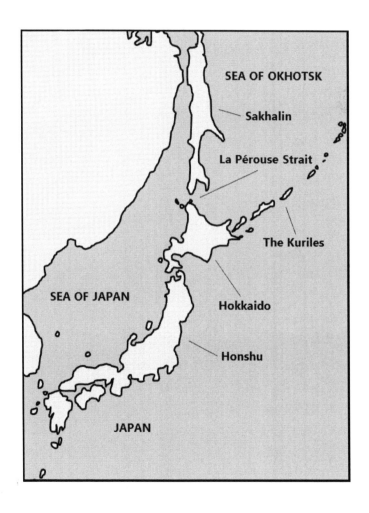

CHAPTER NINE
SUICIDE MISSION

A thousand miles out from Hawaii, sudden squalls churned up swells. *Sandtiger* bobbed across the whitecaps. Below decks, Charlie felt the boat's rhythmic pitch as he finished his daily inspection of the departments.

Another 500 miles, *Sandtiger* would reach Midway and top up their tanks. Ten days later, she'd make landfall at the Kuriles.

Beyond, La Pérouse Strait.

The chiefs reported no problems with the boat. As XO, Charlie enjoyed the view behind the curtain. No, not just a view. Now he was one of the men pulling the levers to keep the magic show going.

As Charlie finished his inspection, he made sure to check the pulse of an essential part of the boat's machinery: the crew's temper. The captain had read the operations order over the 1MC. Whatever fears they might have, the sailors trusted Uncle Charlie (Admiral Lockwood), and they had faith in Moreau. Many seemed downright excited at the prospect of adventure. They were taking the fight straight to the Japanese on their own turf.

Sandtiger, named for a cousin of the great white shark, itched for a fight.

Charlie paused to watch a few dozen sailors finish their meals around the four tables bolted to the mess deck. In the galley, coffee brewed by the gallon. The rest of the crew manned their stations or lounged in their berths, playing acey-deucey and reading cheap paperbacks. "Praise the Lord and Pass the Ammunition," a crew favorite, piped over the loudspeakers. The pharmacist's mate hustled past on his rounds, handing out vitamins to the sun-starved sailors.

There was just one thing missing. Machinist's Mate John Braddock. Charlie smiled. The boat felt a lot roomier without Braddock around.

Satisfied with *Sandtiger*'s morale and efficiency, he headed to the wardroom for coffee. Liebold and Nixon played cribbage at the table. Percy sat on one of the chairs wearing a loud aloha shirt and picking at a banjo. A lit cigarette burned in an ashtray next to him.

"Hey, Harrison, dig this." He plucked the fifth string and produced a lingering G note. Waited four seconds, plucked it again.

Charlie poured himself a mug and grabbed a chair. "What is that?"

"Wait for it." The communications officer grinned and hit another G. Then another—

"Sonar," Nixon said. He cut the pack of cards and flipped one over. "Ha, 'His Heels'! I peg two points for that."

"Good for you," Liebold said in a sulky tone.

Charlie frowned. Liebold had been sour ever since Mare Island. He'd rebuffed every attempt Charlie had made at real conversation.

"Yeah, good one, showoff," Percy said. "You shouldn't play cards with him, Liebold. He's a human computer." He pounded out a first-string D, D, D, D, D—

"Battle stations," Charlie guessed.

"Of course, Harrison gets that one." He played fourth-string D, fifth-string G, third-string G—

"Dive, dive, dive," Nixon said and put down a card. "Thirty-one, Jack."

"*Ah-oo-gah*," Percy said and played it again as chords. "So what do you make of our little mission to the Bathtub, Harrison?"

Charlie sipped his joe. "ComSubPac knows what he's doing."

"It's a suicide mission," Liebold said.

Percy laughed. "Friend, every patrol the captain drags us along on is a suicide mission." He grinned at Charlie. "Why do you think I drink so goddamned hard whenever I can? The Old Man taught me to live each day as if it's my last."

"If it was *my* last day, I'd crap my pants in terror," Nixon noted.

"I love the man, I really do. I'd say I'd follow him to hell and back, but I've already done it."

"We'll be all right," Charlie said, though he didn't

quite believe it. He'd taken enough chances to recognize long odds.

"We all got to go sometime," Percy said. "Pretty soon, we'll have been at war for two years. The jarheads aren't even close to Japan. How long do you think it's going to go on? Another two years? Five? Ten? Do you really think any of us are going home?"

"Don't think like that," Charlie told him. "It'll drive you crazy."

"Or to drink. Mission accomplished."

"You have no idea how close you came to today being your last," Liebold said. "The captain has me modifying the torpedoes two hours a day ever since we left Pearl. One of these days, I'm going to blow us all to hell."

"Is that why you've been so sore?" Charlie wanted to know. "You should be puffing your chest out. What you did allowed us to sink *Yosai*. Sink that destroyer with a down-the-throat shot. You did good."

Liebold threw his cards down. "Yeah. We sank *Yosai*. We did. And *you* got a medal for it. *You* got shipped off to PXO School by Uncle Charlie himself."

"Well, you—"

"Me, I got kicked off *Sabertooth*. Once it got out I messed with torpedoes, nobody wanted me. I only got a posting on *Warmouth* because the exec was my roommate at the Academy. I barely passed my last medical because I stayed in the control room too long breathing in chlorine gas." His face turned scarlet. "Now I'm back doing the dirty work so the heroes can earn glory or kill us all chasing it."

Charlie and Nixon stared at Liebold in a stunned silence.

Percy said, "Well, you didn't have to sugar-coat it."

Charlie sighed. "I don't know what to say. I guess I'm sorry. But what you did shortened the war. Then you saved our lives when that destroyer showed up. The Navy may have come down on you, but all that has to count for something."

"It shortened the war. I'm sure it did. With a captain who's as reckless as you, this mission is going to shorten it even more. I'm sure it'll be a big victory in the end. I just don't think any of us are going to live to see it."

"You're the one who said he wanted to get in the war," Charlie growled.

Liebold stood. "You know what else? The torpedoes Hunter shot down that DD's throat and sank him, they weren't modified. Think about that."

He stormed out.

"Come on, Jack," Charlie called after him.

"Um," Nixon said to fill the awkward silence.

"You make friends everywhere you go, Harrison," Percy said.

"Give it to me straight, fellas. Is the captain reckless?"

"He fights like he plays poker," Nixon said. "Close to the chest, then all-in."

"He gets results," Percy added. "That's all anybody cares about." He strummed a random series of chords that settled into a Gene Autry tune. "Otherwise, nobody gives a damn what I think."

"He seems aggressive to me, but not reckless. You also made out the captain to be some kind of tyrant. So far, he hasn't been the least bit disagreeable to me."

"Because nothing's gone wrong yet," Nixon said. "Watch out for the chiefs."

Charlie set down his coffee, which had gone cold. "What's that supposed to mean? Are they running me down to the captain behind my back?"

"They're more scared of the captain than they are of the Japs," the engineering officer said. "So if anybody screws up, they hide it. The exec always thinks everything is running like a top, but it isn't. Any of those foul-ups affect us in combat, well, it'll be your neck. Maybe mine next time, too."

"For God's sake," Charlie said. "I thought we were fighting the Japanese."

He stood and went to the control room. He put on oilskins, Mae West lifejacket, and sou'wester hat. Then he mounted to the bridge to breathe real air.

The gray sky lay heavy on roiling seas. Waves boomed against the bow, flinging spray across the drenched lookouts. To the north, a line of thunderstorms chased the wind, pounding east toward Canada. Thunder boomed far away, like a remote naval battle. Lightning flashed in the murk.

Charlie looked up at the Mae Wests hanging from the shears. Moreau dived the boat every morning for trim but otherwise kept to the surface at all times, zigging and zagging. The only other time he dived was if an enemy approached within six miles. Then he dived, and he dived in twenty-eight seconds flat. To do that, he reduced the number of lookouts to two and put up the Mae Wests. If anybody failed to get below in time, the captain left him behind and picked him up later.

Maybe Moreau was reckless. This mission certainly felt reckless. One thing was for sure, the captain didn't let anything stand in the way of killing the hated Japanese. If the boat experienced a failure in combat Charlie hadn't anticipated, Moreau would see him as being in the way. And he'd crush him for it.

Charlie had wanted to return to the war because things seemed simpler out here.

He couldn't have been more wrong.

CHAPTER TEN

THE STRAIT

Two weeks later, Charlie stood on the bridge, wearing a muffler, coat, and boots. The Sea of Okhotsk lay cold and calm in the moonless night, hidden by a veil of fog. The black shapes of the Kuriles loomed astern.

The Kuriles reached 800 miles from Hokkaido to Kamchatka. Cruising north by northwest, *Sandtiger* slipped through this first line of defense after sunset. She'd raced pell-mell between Iturup and Urup with her throttles wide open. Boxed in by hostile landmasses, she was now in Japanese waters, making way across the cold sea.

"Conn, Bridge," Captain Moreau said. "Come left to two-seven-oh."

"Come left to two-seven-oh, aye, Captain."

Sandtiger was first in line to go through the strait. The captain wouldn't have it any other way. Somewhere astern, *Warmouth* followed in the fog. As the flagship, *Redhorse* went last.

Percy scanned the dark with his binoculars. "Christ, it's cold. Hey Skipper, don't the Japs know it's August?"

"Lucky it's summer," the captain said. "La Pérouse freezes up a good part of the year."

Charlie stiffened. A tiny blob of light glimmered through the fog. "Ship, ahoy! On the starboard beam. He's got his running lights on."

Moreau trained his binoculars on the light and grunted. "Looks like our good friends, the Reds."

The United States and Soviet Union were allies against the Axis. Food, raw materials, and non-military goods flowed into the USSR via the Pacific Route. From West Coast ports riding up the Aleutians and down the Kuriles. Then through La Pérouse to the port of Vladivostok.

"The enemy of my enemy is my friend," Percy said, quoting an old proverb.

Moreau: "Sugar Jig, make an automatic sweep on the PPI."

Overhead, the radar swiveled as it swept the sea.

The blob of light grew larger. The submarine and the mystery ship were on a convergent course.

"Ship contact, bearing two-four-five, double-oh-five on the starboard bow, range two miles," the SJ radarman reported. "Second ship contact, bearing two-four-five, oh-one-oh on the starboard bow, 2,000 yards."

Damn it, that was close. Charlie zeroed in with his binoculars but didn't see the second ship through the fog.

"Helm, reduce speed to one-third," Moreau snarled. He didn't like surprises. He wanted to put a little distance between them.

"Jap, you think?" Percy asked.

"Maybe. Or maybe a Red captain too dumb to remember to turn his lights on. It don't change a thing. We're going in."

A freezing southerly blew over the water, disturbing its calm. Charlie rubbed his gloved hands over his numb face to warm it up and returned the binoculars to his eyes. The blob of light crossed the starboard bow, followed by its companion.

"Helm, Bridge," Moreau barked. "All ahead full."

Sandtiger knifed the sea in hot pursuit of the two ships. One of the lookouts spotted another lighted ship off the starboard quarter.

Moreau could wait and hitch a ride behind the new arrival, but he wanted to get through the strait by sunrise. Every minute counted.

"Helm, come right to two-eight-five."

The hours rolled by. Charlie and Percy stomped their feet on the icy deck to get their blood pumping. *Sandtiger* made way at nineteen knots toward the strait.

Ahead, the blob of light dimmed.

"We're losing him," Charlie said.

The fog was thickening.

Ahead lay another danger, Nijogan Rock, largest among an islet group off Sakhalin. Just 500 feet long and 150 feet wide, it presented a hazard to ships traveling the strait. The Russians called it "Dangerous Rock" for obvious reasons. If *Sandtiger* ran aground, the rock would rip her hull wide open.

Moreau rubbed his hands to warm them. "Helm, come left to two-seven-oh."

Pea-soup fog enveloped the boat, and Charlie went blind.

"'Abandon hope, all ye who enter here,'" Percy said, quoting *Dante's Inferno*.

Charlie felt the same foreboding. They headed into dangerous, unknown waters. In May, the *Pickerel* was presumed lost just on the other side of the Kuriles, off the coast of Hokkaido.

As with other submarine losses during the war, nobody knew what happened. The boat never came home. It simply disappeared.

Another blob of light. "Captain, ship off the starboard bow!"

Sandtiger was off course!

Way off course, in fact. Moreau had turned due west too early. *Sandtiger* now headed straight into the minefields hemming the safe channel.

"That's Nijogan," Moreau growled. "The Reds keep a lighthouse on it."

Percy snorted.

"Ah, right," Charlie said. Shit. He'd been about to recommend conning *Sandtiger* north. Right into it.

Moreau: "Sugar Jig, give me another sweep on the PPI."

A minute later, the conning tower reported, "The radar's down, Captain."

"Uh-huh," the captain seethed.

"I'll go, sir," Charlie said.

"Stay at your station. Nixon's on it."

The boat labored to make way, her speed diminishing. The strait's powerful current flowed east during the summer.

"Contact!" Charlie said. "Three-five-oh on the port bow. He's lighted."

The ship appeared to be heading due east.

"Keep her so," Moreau ordered the helmsman.

Sandtiger maintained her heading. The Russian ship steamed past, lights burning in the inky blackness.

Nixon's voice over the intercom: "Sugar Jig back in operation, Captain."

A blown fuse, probably. Amazing how equipment always seemed to fail when needed most. At least this breakdown had a simple fix.

"Very well! Now give me a damn sweep!"

Radar revealed landmasses around them. Nijogan and Sakhalin to the northwest, Hokkaido to the southeast. Ships coming and going.

Sandtiger entered La Pérouse.

"In the old days," said Moreau, "a ship's crew listened for the sea lions making a ruckus on the rock. That's how they knew where Nijogan was."

"That's interesting," Percy said in breathless terror.

Right now, the submarine was passing through the minefields. The mines swayed in the black depths, waiting.

If the captain felt scared, he didn't show it. He didn't seem to experience fear, only impatience. "Conn, Bridge. Time check."

Sunrise was coming fast.

The fog might protect them. It might not. *Sandtiger* had to submerge soon, but first she had to clear the minefields.

The submarine slowed a little, labored a little harder to make way. The Soviet ship ahead blew his foghorn. The ship astern answered.

Charlie had a thought. "Captain, the safe channel may not be mined above a depth of seventy feet."

"How do you figure?"

"The Japs are going out of their way not to anger Stalin. A depth of forty feet is only a five-foot margin of error. They wouldn't risk sinking a Russian ship. I think they mined the channel at seventy feet. We might submerge if we had to."

At periscope depth, the submarine reached a depth of sixty-five feet, five above the horned mines floating in the deep. A close shave, but at least they'd be underwater and out of sight.

"Maybe," the captain said. "Don't think we'll have to dive in any case."

Dawn brightened the sky. The hair-raising ride across the Sea of Okhotsk had taken all night, though it'd gone by in a flash.

The fog thinned to wisps as *Sandtiger* left the strait.

"Ship ahoy, dead ahead," Charlie said. He'd found the ship that had its lights off during the passage. "Russian fishing trawler."

Otherwise, the open sea looked clear in the growing daylight.

"The holy of holies," Moreau said.

The green-blue waters of the Sea of Japan. Clouds formed a remarkable zigzag pattern overhead, burned orange by the rising sun.

"We made it," Percy sighed. "Thank you, sweet baby Jesus."

Operation Payback had begun.

CHAPTER ELEVEN

THE BOTTOM OF THE SEA

Charlie slid down the ladder to the conning tower. He stowed his coat and muffler and rubbed his arms to get warm.

The captain came down minutes later. "You get the message off, Charlie?"

The wolf pack used a special new code Cooper's people cooked up to shorten communications between the boats. Shorter messages gave the Japanese less time to detect and zero in on the signals.

"Message sent and confirmed both ways," Charlie said. "*Warmouth* and *Redhorse* both say they made it across."

The operation was off to a good start. *Sandtiger* could now rest while the other submarines moved on to their hunting grounds. *Sandtiger* would cover the western coast of Hokkaido. *Redhorse*, the mid-sea between Dogo and northern Honshu. *Warmouth*, the sea's southern end.

"Very well." Moreau pulled out his battered lawn chair and sat in it with a contented sigh. "Time to pull the plug."

"Aye, aye." Charlie keyed the 1MC call box. "Rig for dive. Clear the bridge."

The lookouts zipped down the ladder. Percy called out, "Hatch secured!"

"Dive, dive, dive!"

The klaxon blasted twice.

Sandtiger had a different layout than the S-55 and *Sabertooth*. In those boats, attack, navigation, diving, and control all happened in the control room. In *Sandtiger*, the conning tower served as the CO's battle and navigation center. Just eight feet wide by seventeen feet long, the conn packed up to ten men at stations during combat.

The TDC aft to port, the radar stations aft to starboard. Sonar just forward of the TDC. Plotting table, periscopes, torpedo indicator panels. The helmsman steered the boat at his station mounted against the forward bulkhead.

Chief of the Boat "Spike" Sullivan oversaw operations in the control room below. The planes, manifold, and instrumentation such as the gyrocompass, fathometer, and bathythermograph.

"Maneuvering, stop the main engines," Charlie said. "Switch to battery power. Control, rig out the bow planes. Close the main induction."

In the maneuvering room, electricians took the motors off engine power and put them on battery power. The main induction, which fed air to the engines, banged shut. The bow planes extended from the hull.

"Helm, all ahead two-thirds."

"All ahead two-thirds, aye, Exec." The helmsman rang up the designated speed.

"Pressure in the boat, green board," Spike shouted up from the control room. "The boat is rigged for dive!"

The green and red lights on the Christmas Tree showed all hull openings secured. Air pressure flowed within the hull, confirming the boat was sealed.

"Fathometer reading?"

"One-nine-five, Exec."

"Very well." Charlie turned to Moreau. "Ready to dive in all respects, Captain. The boat has 195 feet under the keel."

The captain nodded with a distant smile. He seemed to be listening to the boat talk to him, sensing every part of her. "Dive."

"Aye, aye. Control, open all main vents. Flood safety. Flood negative."

In the control room below, the hydraulic manifoldman pulled a vent valve lever. This opened the main ballast tanks, which were filled with air to maintain buoyancy on the surface. Seawater flooded them, which made the boat heavy.

Moreau said, "Take us down and set her like a baby on the bottom."

The submarine's bow slid into the sea as she angled down on propulsion. The air pressure increased in Charlie's ears. He watched the depth gauge. The needle crept around the dial as *Sandtiger* sought the deep.

"Depth, forty-five feet," Charlie said. "Control, close all vents."

At 180 feet, he ordered the negative tank blown to restore buoyancy. Charlie's shoulders clenched with tension. Percy grabbed the nearest handhold. Moreau sat in his sagging chair with his hands folded on his belly. Calm as Buddha. He operated on his gut, and his gut hadn't been wrong yet.

"Speed one-third, Captain."

"Very well. Control, ease your bubble."

Sandtiger glided onto the sea bottom.

"All stop," said Moreau.

The boat nestled on an even keel, her screws stopped.

"Final depth, one-nine-seven," Charlie sighed. "Control, open bulkhead flappers. Start the ventilation."

Moreau gripped the armrests and heaved himself up with a grunt. "Section three will report to stations." He said to the quartermaster, "Smokey, the conn is yours. Everybody else should get some rest. We got a busy four days ahead of us."

"Might be a good time to splice the mainbrace," Percy ventured.

The captain smiled. "I got something even better in mind. A fresh education. You too, Charlie. Tell Nixon to meet us in the wardroom. Dat sourpuss Liebold can mind the store while we're gone."

Charlie pulled Percy aside. "What's going on?"

The communications officer groaned. "The Old Man wants to play poker."

CHAPTER TWELVE

ALL IN

The weary officers shuffled into the wardroom for a few hands of poker. A good game for submariners. Luck, probability, and high stakes. Shuffling cards at the table, Moreau eyed them like the shark after which the boat was named.

Good idea, Charlie thought. *Some coffee to heat me up. Something to take my mind off my claustrophobia.*

Not quite claustrophobia. He'd looked up the precise word. *Cleithrophobia.* The fear of being trapped.

Some guys puked their guts out while at sea. Not Charlie, not even when the boat listed up to thirty degrees a side during a severe storm. Raised among sailboats, he had strong sea legs, never stumbled on deck. When the submarine rode the surface, he slept like a baby while the great engines sang to him through the hull.

Underwater, he felt trapped. Buried alive, to be exact.

The unease started during the dive. Dry mouth, sweaty hands. He'd pictured the waves cascading across the deck as she sank. As the boat submerged, he thought about the endless tons of water pressing against the hull.

By the time *Sandtiger* touched the bottom, his heart thumped like it would burst right out of his chest.

Moreau said, "Grab a chair, gents. The game is Texas hold 'em."

The captain dealt two cards to each man. Waldron, the steward's mate, served hot coffee all around.

Charlie picked up a red checker from the stack in front of him. Ten boxes of the game lay piled under the table. "You play for checkers?"

"Worth a penny each," Moreau said. "We settle up at the end of the patrol."

A soundman had taught Charlie the game when he served on the 55. The auxiliarymen had fleeced him until he learned how to play well.

Percy put down a checker as the blind. Charlie, two checkers as the big blind. He held a jack and ten of spades as hole cards, a hand with decent prospects. The officers all put in bets, two checkers each.

The captain laid down the flop from the deck, three face-up cards. The ten of hearts, king of spades, and queen of spades.

The idea was to put together the best five-card poker hand using both his hole cards and the face-up community cards. With the two tens, Charlie had a pair. Not exactly a winning hand, but better than nothing.

As dealer, Moreau would put down another face-up card after the next round of betting, called "the turn." Then another after that, called "the river."

If the ace of spades showed, Charlie would have a royal flush. An unbeatable hand. He had two chances to get it.

The probability of the deck producing that card was miniscule, though.

Otherwise, he had good odds at getting a king-high flush, since he already had four spades. A straight flush, full house, and four of a kind beat it, but it was still an excellent hand. He also had a crack at a straight if any ace turned up. Four of a kind with his two tens if by some miracle the next two cards were tens.

Moreau raised his bet. "I do believe I'll have my cigar now." He produced a fat stogie from his breast pocket and lit up with a cloud of acrid smoke. Percy joined him, torching one of his Lucky Strikes.

The captain's ashtray was a twisted chunk of metal that had landed topside after he blew a freighter sky high off the coast of Borneo.

Nixon's eyes flickered across the cards as he performed rapid probability calculations. He frowned as he carefully laid down his checkers. "I call."

"Mother of God, boy," Moreau said. "You got more tells than a cat in heat."

Percy said, "Behold my blank face and neutral body language."

"Ha," Moreau said. "I can still read you, Jerry. You got nothin'."

"Oh, you're right." He set his cards down. "I fold. You want me to be more aggressive, Skipper, we should play for booze."

"What about you, sunshine? You gonna check?"

Charlie's heart hammered in his chest. The cleithrophobia was worse knowing the boat lay on the bottom of the sea, engines off. He blew air out his cheeks. "No, I'll raise."

The captain frowned behind a cloud of cigar smoke. "You're bluffing." He called. Then he turned the next community card.

The two of clubs.

Nixon folded with a sigh.

Charlie raised again. He still had very good odds at a flush.

Moreau grinned. "Looks like we got ourselves a showdown. You're still bluffing. Look at your face, rigged for red. Here comes the river."

Five of spades.

No royal flush, but he'd gotten his flush.

"I'll raise," the captain said.

Charlie called and laid out his cards. "Flush, king high."

Moreau grunted, his face darkening. "Jack-high straight. Well, look at dat."

"Congratulations, Harrison," Percy said, grinding out his smoke in the ashtray. "Looks like you're buying, next time we're in port."

"I have to admit, I read you wrong," the captain said. "Sitting there red-faced and sweating buckets."

The cleithrophobia had screwed up the captain's radar. But Charlie couldn't tell him that.

He pulled the stack of checkers in front of him. "I was raising my bets on the small chance you'd turn the ace and give me a royal flush. The flush was my main hope. The odds were good enough you'd pull a spade."

"You can tell a lot about a man the way he plays poker. Look at Nixon here. He can drum up probabilities like a human TDC, but he hates taking chances. You? You play like you fight. Going on Mindanao to shoot Japs. Drilling *Yosai* in a surface attack. You go all in."

Again, the truth was somewhat different. Going ashore at Mindanao had almost gotten him and Braddock killed. Taking on *Yosai* had also been rash with battle damage that nearly prevented the boat from diving.

In the strait, he'd confused Nijogan Rock with the Russian running lights. Instead of querying for a radar sweep, he'd concluded *Sandtiger* was off course. Quiet Bill had been right to worry about his experience. Lewis, Charlie's last XO, had said a good submariner had to be both willing *and* able.

"A submarine attack is a lot like high-stakes poker," Moreau said. "You start with a stack of chips. Concealment, surprise, torpedoes, battery power, air. Your very lives. You gamble them one at a time to win. Some men fold early. Others, if the pot is big enough, they gamble it all. You're a gambler, Charlie."

Charlie stared at the captain and wondered. *Am I like you?*

The captain collected the cards and shuffled them. Then he dealt again.

CHAPTER THIRTEEN

THE HUNT

Sunset.

Sandtiger shuddered as she left the ocean floor and rose to a depth of sixty-five feet.

There, she glided with a one-degree up bubble.

Moreau heaved himself from his lawn chair and jerked his thumbs. At the unspoken command, the periscope rose from its well. He yanked the handles down and pressed his wide face against the rubber eyepiece.

"Uh-huh," he grunted. "Fog all over. Down scope. Sugar Jig, do a sweep."

The radarman called out contacts. Land masses, no ships. According to the maps, Rebun and Rishiri lay to the west and southwest. East was Hokkaido, the northernmost of the Japanese Home Islands.

On these islands, millions of people labored around the clock to support a war effort that had won them one-tenth of the world.

Moreau: "Let's take her up, Charlie."

"Aye, aye, Captain." Charlie keyed the 1MC. "All compartments, rig to surface."

The men in the conning tower smiled at the command, even the taciturn Liebold. They'd come halfway around the world. At midnight, the wolf pack would start hunting Japanese ships in their own backyard.

"Maneuvering, stand by to switch from motors to diesels," Charlie said. "On surfacing, answer bells on the main engines. Put two mains on charge."

Once *Sandtiger* reached the surface, the electricians would uncouple the electric motors from the batteries and put them on the diesels. Two engines would power the boat while the other two dumped amps into the waning batteries.

The telephone talker relayed the order to Maneuvering.

"Forward engine room, secure ventilation," Charlie said. "All compartments, shut the bulkhead flappers."

"All compartments report rigged to surface," the telephone talker said.

Charlie turned toward Moreau. "Ready to surface in every respect, Captain."

Him, most of all. Constant work had kept the cleithrophobia at bay so far, but he craved an unsecured hatch. A way out of this cramped metal box.

"Very well. Take her up."

His heart flooded with relief as the surfacing alarm blared. "Control, blow all main ballast tanks. Blow negative."

High-pressure air poured into the ballast tanks, displacing the water and buoying the boat. The planesmen angled the boat into a controlled ascent.

Charlie pulled on a windbreaker and hung binoculars from his neck. *Sandtiger* didn't rig for red. Instead, he pulled on red goggles that would help him adapt more quickly to night vision. "Lookouts, report to the tower."

Smokey and two sailors showed up for the watch and got ready. *Sandtiger* burst from the sea. The quartermaster undogged the hatch and cracked it open. Air whistled from the boat in a rush as the pressure equalized.

Grateful to be back in the open air, Charlie mounted to the bridge. He scanned the darkness with his binoculars but didn't see anything through the close-aboard fog. Still, their position was secure enough. The radar could see what he couldn't.

"All clear!" he called down.

The men piled out and took their watch stations. The engines fired.

Charlie grinned. "Welcome to Area One."

"Land of the Rising Sun," Smokey said. "Land of the Fog is more like it."

"Damn chilly too," one of the lookouts grumbled. "Supposed to be August."

A cool breeze blew from the north. The air temperature was sixty degrees.

Sandtiger turned to port, heading south into the Rishiri Channel.

"Lights, Mr. Harrison," the quartermaster said. "Three-four-oh on the port bow."

"A town. Teshio, I think. Just a fishing village."

"Look at them, with their lights on."

"Oil lamps and the like, probably."

"Any lamps, sir. The town should be dark. Either there are no blackout rules, or nobody is following them. It's like they don't know there's a war on."

Charlie said, "We'll take it, Smokey."

"Hey, I'm not complaining. Makes it easier to navigate."

"We'll hug the coast a bit and see what turns up. The captain wants to make a run down to Rumoi, a fishing center. Maybe we'll find some shipping there."

"We're supposed to wait until midnight before we shoot anything, right?"

Charlie shrugged. Only the captain knew his own mind. The Old Man certainly didn't like taking orders from Rickard. Very likely, he was itching to sink the first ship. It was all moot, though, until he found that ship.

At 2130, *Sandtiger* prowled outside Rumoi. Two jetties protected the harbor from foul weather. A lighthouse gleamed at the end of each of these breakwaters.

"Fishing boats," Smokey said with disappointment.

Charlie's eyes strained to penetrate the darkness. "Your night vision is better than mine. I don't see them."

"Trust me. Fishing boats."

"I see them now." Charlie relayed the information to the conn. Moreau growled something in response. Moments later, *Sandtiger* turned to starboard and continued her southward trek along Hokkaido's coast.

Tedium was part of war. He understood that well. Patience was at the heart of submarining. Wait and hurry up. This time, however, they only had four days.

They'd come all this way, taken all this risk, to wreak havoc.

Sandtiger rounded Iwao and returned to a southerly heading at eighteen knots. The coastline was black as far as the eye could see, sparsely inhabited. Rollers dashed against the rocky shore.

"Smokey, you've served with the captain a long time," Charlie said.

"I was on *Sandtiger* before he was," the quartermaster said.

Best to come right out with it. "He goes through a lot of execs."

He sensed Smokey grinning in the dark. "He sure does."

"The dope is the chiefs are scared of him, so they hide big malfunctions. Then if anything goes wrong in combat, the exec takes the heat. Gets on the Old Man's bad side."

The quartermaster laughed. "Right."

"Why are you laughing?"

"Because it's a giant load of horseshit, sir."

"Well, what gives?"

"You looking for advice, Mr. Harrison?"

Charlie wasn't sure. As XO, he couldn't express any uncertainty about his job. But he needed to learn. "I'll always take advice from a sea dog."

"Don't hold anything back. Attack the Japs with everything you've got."

"I think I follow."

"The captain knows you haven't been in the boats that long. He doesn't care. He wants a fighter, somebody who thinks like him."

Again, Charlie wondered if he and the captain were alike. "Thanks, Smokey."

"You'll be all right."

The fog thinned as they crossed Ishikari Bay and approached the city of Otaru. The sprawling port had impressive breakwaters flung wide across the bay. As with Teshio and Rumoi, lights burned in the city.

Japanese merchant ships lay moored in a series of wharfs.

"Now we're talking," the quartermaster said.

"Marus," Charlie said. "And one big ship that could be a sea tender."

"No warships, though. Not that I spy."

"Ship off the starboard quarter, far!" one of the lookouts called out.

Charlie searched for it. "You see him, Smokey?"

"Looks like a small freighter coming home from Manchuria."

"I've got him now. Conn, Bridge. Contact, ship, likely a small freighter, bearing one-five-oh. One-double-oh on the starboard quarter. He rounded Takashima and is heading for Otaru."

He checked the time. Fifteen minutes before midnight. The operations order didn't allow *Sandtiger* to shoot, but Moreau would likely see it as close enough. Heading directly toward an American submarine, the freighter was small but easy pickings. A perfect start to the mission.

"We're going to let him pass," Moreau responded on the intercom.

Charlie and Smokey exchanged a wondering glance.

"First time I ever saw the Old Man leave food on the table," the quartermaster murmured. "Something's up."

"Captain," Charlie said into the intercom, "I suggest—"

"Forget him, Charlie. We just got a message from *Redhorse*. We have bigger fish to fry tonight. Much bigger fish."

Sandtiger plowed the waters as she turned and made for the open sea.

CHAPTER FOURTEEN
RICKARD'S RAIDERS

The conning tower buzzed with excitement. *Redhorse* had found a convoy of troop transports. Eight ships in all. Steaming at ten knots, no zigzagging.

Four civilian passenger-cargo ships and two ocean liners. All converted to military transport and big enough to move an entire division. Weapons, munitions, parts, stores. Maybe even tanks and crated airplanes.

Two escorts. A *Fubuki* and an old *Momi*-type DD.

Captain Rickard trailed them with his *Redhorse*. He might sink one or two before the destroyers barreled after him. He hoped to sink them all in a single strike, so he alerted the wolf pack.

But they were far away.

Charlie, Moreau, Percy, and Nixon studied the map at the plotting table in the conning tower. A line extended from Hokkaido toward the center of the Sea of Japan. *Sandtiger*.

A second line reached northwest from the port of Niigata in central Honshu.

"The convoy appears to be headed for Seishin,"

Moreau said. A Korean port.

"Replacements for the Kwantung Army," Charlie guessed.

The Kwantung Army guarded Manchuria against Soviet invasion. Its ranks included the best units in the Imperial Japanese Army.

Moreau grunted. "Don't matter. What matters is, if they're going to Seishin, they're gonna cross the middle of the Japan Sea. We're in the game."

"It's a hell of a long way," Percy said. His aloha shirt glared red and yellow in the conning tower's light. Charlie wondered why the captain allowed him to break the uniform regulations. Maybe neither of them cared.

The yeoman approached. "Decoded message from *Redhorse*, Captain."

Moreau read the message and handed it to Percy. "The good commodore has given us the coordinates where he hopes to attack at 0130 tomorrow. Our objective is to sink all six troopships in a decisive night surface attack."

Standard submarine doctrine. Describe the target, how to sink it.

Charlie checked his watch. About 25 hours.

Rickard knew his wolf pack tactics, which the German U-boats had perfected as the war progressed. The first submarine on the scene acted as the shadow, staying out of sight while keeping contact with the convoy. When other submarines arrived, the coordinator gave the signal to attack. The result was devastating.

The communications officer marked the overlay with an X using a grease pencil. The spot was about 350 miles from Niigata.

Charlie blinked at the plot. "That's out of range!"

Up to the attack area, the convoy had to travel 250 miles. *Sandtiger*, 350. The submarine made eighteen knots, the transports ten. At dawn, however, *Sandtiger* submerged. Underwater, she made only three knots.

Percy scratched his head. "We're short, what, about seventy miles?"

"Sixty-eight miles to be exact," Nixon said.

Moreau said, "We're gonna stay on the surface in daylight."

Charlie and Percy exchanged a horrified glance.

"On the surface," Percy clarified. "In daylight. In the Sea of Japan."

"I don't believe in ideal setups any more than I do Santa Claus. Dis is the only way to do it. We'll dive at any sign of trouble." The captain's eyes narrowed under bushy eyebrows. "Only gonna ask you boys once. You with me?"

Percy looked away as if searching for a good spot to throw up. "All the way, Captain. Only way to do it."

Charlie again wondered if Moreau was bold or mad. "Aye, Captain."

"Yes, Captain," Nixon said.

"Uh-huh," said the captain.

"We don't have to stay surfaced the whole way," Charlie said.

"Two hours, forty-eight minutes," Nixon said. "That's how long."

"You're looking at it wrong," Moreau said. "We're going on the surface. The whole run. We have nine hours we can be submerged if we have to pull the plug."

Charlie studied the map but saw no other option. A daylight run was possible. The main variable was how long they could cruise on the surface. A variable they couldn't even guess. They didn't know the territory.

A big risk, yes, but for a gigantic reward.

The six troop transports carried what might be an entire division. Ten thousand men and all their equipment. They'd have an artillery regiment aboard.

Sinking these ships and their cargo would be a major blow against the Japanese. Some opportunities, you just can't pass up.

"*Redhorse* will update us if anything changes," Moreau said. "Charlie, during the attack, you'll be on the bridge with me. I want you on the TBT."

The captain wanted them to work together as a team to take down the transports. Surprised, Charlie again gave the only permissible answer: "Aye, Captain."

"I command. You execute. You make all observations. All right?"

Was he kidding? "It's music to my ears, Captain."

"I thought you might say that." Moreau turned and barked, "Helmsman, come right to two-four-five. Jerry will give you the coordinates. Set a new course as the crow flies."

"Come right to two-four-five, aye, Captain," the helmsman answered.

The captain pulled down the 1MC handset and keyed the callbox for public address. "Listen up, crew. This is your captain."

His voice blared over the loudspeakers. Across *Sandtiger*, the sailors stopped and listened.

"By now, you may have heard we just passed up a beauty steaming into Otaru Harbor. He would have made a nice patch on our flag. We're after much bigger fish now. We're after Moby Dick himself. You see, Cap'n Rickard decided Christmas should come early this year."

Moreau paused to let their imaginations run wild. "Ol' Rick found us a convoy of eight tin cans. Six of 'em troopships big enough to haul a division. We do dis right, we'll have a lot of patches on our flag. Just to make things more exciting and so we get there on time, we're gonna make the run in daylight. Depending on the traffic above water, our girl might get a lot of exercise today. Stay sharp, do your duty, and let's bag those cans. We're gonna hit the Japs where they live. Show 'em nowhere is safe." He paused again. "Dat's all, I guess."

He returned the handset as the crew cheered across the boat.

CHAPTER FIFTEEN

DOUBLE OR NOTHING

Four hours before dawn. Last chance for rest before *Sandtiger*'s daylight run across the Japan Sea.

Charlie collapsed on his bunk and pulled the blanket over his shoulder. Too much to think about. Too little time to rest before the harrowing day ahead.

Percy hauled himself up onto the overhead bunk. After a few minutes, he asked Charlie if he was awake.

Charlie didn't answer, stubbornly trying to cross over.

"Hey. Hey, Harrison. *Harrison*."

"What?" he cried.

"You awake?"

"What do you want, Percy?"

"I was wondering what you like to do for fun."

"I like to sleep," Charlie growled. "We've only got four hours."

"Come on, man. Talk to me a little. I get insomnia."

"Worried about running the sea in broad daylight? Is that it?"

"No. I mean, yeah. Of course."

"We're all worried, Percy."

"I wonder if guys on Death Row get a good night's rest before the electric chair. I doubt it."

"The captain knows what he's doing." The statement had become mere reflex by this point.

"I've served with him longer than you," Percy said. "He has a keen eye for the odds, I'll give him that. He hates the Japs more than any man alive does. Every time he wins, though, he ups his bets. Pushes the odds. Hates the Japs even more. I hope it doesn't catch up to him. Seeing as we're all in the same boat."

Charlie said nothing. Submarine commanders like Moreau were innovating new doctrine. Achieving great successes. The old doctrine certainly wasn't accomplishing a whole lot in this war. Between timid commanders and faulty torpedoes, the Japanese barely regarded the submarines as a threat.

Moreau liked to fight on the surface at night. Patrol on the surface during daylight hours and dive only when the enemy was within six miles. Use radar instead of passive sonar for tracking and targeting. Allow his XO to make combat observations while he conned the boat and focused on the battle. Keep the periscope up longer and more often when submerged.

And always attack, attack, attack.

The captain took big risks but achieved even bigger results. Charlie trusted him. He wanted to trust him. Wanted to believe reason, not blind hatred, drove Moreau's boldness. If reason, the man was possibly a genius. If hatred, he was a madman who might get them all killed.

Percy said, "The reason I can't sleep sometimes is I think about home so hard I start to believe I might get there again. Then I get the bad dreams."

Charlie propped himself on his elbow. "What sort of dreams? The boat sinking, that kind of thing?"

Percy sighed. "I dream I go home, and I know it's where I grew up, but everything's different. All the houses are different. Nobody knows me. My family and friends, nobody. I tell them who I am, but they say they never heard of me. They ask me if I was in the war, and I say yes, I served on *Sandtiger* in the Pacific. They just stare at me with this sad, scared look on their faces. That's when I realize I'm dead. I died in the war. Then I wake up."

"Shit," Charlie said. "That's a rough one. I dream about the Japanese."

"On the level?"

"I see them screaming in the water. Eyes looking at me from faces covered in oil. Clothes blown off by the blast. The sea on fire."

"Shit," Percy said.

"Yeah. Shit."

In other dreams, he relived the fight with the *Mizukaze*. Bodies of the deck gun crew flew apart under cannon fire. Captain Hunter said, "Very well," just before the conning tower exploded in a blinding flash.

Shit.

"So what do you like to do for fun?" Percy said.

Charlie enjoyed doing many things, but he couldn't name something he did just for fun. He'd grown up without a father during the hard times of the Depression. Work was all he knew as long as he could remember.

He said, "Hang out with my girl, I guess."

"The hot little number at the dance hall?"

"That's Evie. There's also Jane, an Army nurse."

The mattress rustled overhead. Percy peered over the edge of the bed, looking at Charlie upside-down. "You have two girls."

"The truth is I don't really have either one of them."

"Yeah, I understand. But you have *two girls*." Percy's face disappeared. The mattress rustled again as the man settled on his back. "Never would have pictured you juggling the ladies, Harrison. You strike me as the earnest family type."

"I'll get there eventually."

"Who's it gonna be?"

"Evie reminds me of home. Jane reminds me of the war."

Percy snorted. "Sounds like an easy choice to me."

"You'd be surprised."

"You're an interesting guy, Harrison. I hope you survive all this. Make one of those girls a happy lady."

"You too. So what do you do for fun besides drink and play banjo, Percy?"

"I'm nuts about bowling."

Charlie closed his eyes and listened.

Smokey shook him awake what felt like seconds later.

CHAPTER SIXTEEN

DAYLIGHT RUN

Sandtiger barreled toward the center of Area One in broad daylight.

The orange morning sun set the horizon afire. The sea opal and emerald. Japan a mere smudge on the horizon to port.

Charlie could spare no attention for sightseeing. However striking, the vista was hostile territory. The water home to warships. The clouds perfect camouflage for planes that might come howling from the sky.

From his position on the bridge, he scanned the view with his binoculars. He kept the same reduced number of lookouts but shortened their watch to two hours. While *Sandtiger* ran the gauntlet, he wanted the men to have fresh eyes at all times.

So far, so good. They hadn't had to dive yet.

The lookouts were quiet. None of the typical banter that involved home, women, or riding each other's ass without quarter.

Everybody was on edge today.

One of the sailors called out: "Plane, far, bearing two-eight-oh, elevation four-triple-oh, crossing the stern."

"Very well," Charlie said. No threat.

They'd spotted four planes, all at a far enough distance to cause little worry. Three ships as well, all on the horizon.

Liebold emerged from the hatch with two fresh lookouts. "Permission to relieve you."

"Granted," Charlie said.

The sailors went below as the new lookouts scrambled up the shears.

"You'd better get down below too," Liebold said.

He was right, but Charlie wanted to stick around. He hated the idea of being below decks. Up here, he could see the enemy coming and act.

Sandtiger had been moving in daylight for two hours. Just one more hour, and they could travel submerged the rest of the way if necessary.

"You still sore?" Charlie ventured.

"Leave it alone."

"I will if you quit moping. We need you, Jack."

"What do you want from me? I modified the lousy torpedoes. Every single one."

Charlie shook his head. He couldn't break through. He hated being on the outs with Liebold. The man had been the closest thing he'd had to a friend on *Sabertooth*. He started for the hatch, squinting in the sun's glare.

And jumped.

A black dot in the sun, growing larger.

"Dive!" Charlie shouted into the intercom. "Clear the bridge! Move!"

The men slid down the ladder into the control room. Charlie spun the center wheel to dog the hatch. "Hatch secured!"

He dropped into the conning tower as the boat angled down.

"Plane, approaching, maybe five miles!"

"Take it easy," Moreau said. "Control, take her down, emergency."

Sandtiger clawed toward her test depth of 300 feet.

Charlie grabbed a handhold and looked up. The plane had been far away, but it moved a lot faster than the boat. Recon planes traveled at speeds topping 200 miles an hour. Many carried bombs big enough to smash a hole in a submarine.

Right now, the plane might be zeroing in on the swirling bubbles that marked *Sandtiger*'s plunge into the sea.

"Recommend evasive action, Captain," Charlie said.

"Steady as you go," Moreau replied.

Percy: "Passing 100 feet, Skipper!"

Charlie checked his watch. The plane would have crossed the five-mile distance in forty-five seconds. It should be overhead by now.

"Maybe he didn't have any bombs," he guessed.

"Or didn't see us at all," Percy said.

"Maybe the little bastard saw us and marked our

position with smoke for bombers," Moreau taunted. "Maybe he radioed the nearest naval base, which is now firing tin cans at us. You can maybe yourself right into a straitjacket."

Percy smiled. "Maybe we should focus on what we know?"

Moreau sat in his old lawn chair, which sagged under his weight. "'Atta boy. A plane showed up. We dived. It don't change a thing."

Taking a cue from the captain, the sailors relaxed at their stations. For the next half-hour, though, nobody said anything unrelated to his job. Nixon came to relieve Percy in the conning tower. Again, Charlie stuck around.

Moreau hauled himself to his feet. "Control, bring us back up to periscope depth."

Down in the control room, the planesmen turned the large brass wheels that angled the boat. *Sandtiger* rose toward the surface and leveled off.

The captain raised his thumbs. He hugged the periscope as it rose from its well, slowly rotating for a good look all around.

"We're clear," he said. "Down scope. Rig to surface. Let's get back at it."

"Recommend we keep the negative ballast tanks partially flooded," Charlie said. "It'll slow us down a bit, but we'll be able to dive faster."

Moreau threw him the stink-eye. "Jack's got the watch, Exec. Nixon's doin' the plotting. You're in everybody's way. Go do it somewhere else."

Charlie stormed off to the wardroom for a cup of coffee. Percy strummed his banjo in one of the chairs with his feet propped on another.

"Man, you look like a coiled spring," the communications officer said.

"We're running the Sea of Japan in broad daylight. Every officer should stay on duty in case something goes wrong. I should be assistant diving officer now."

"The Old Man likes to keep it lean."

"Does he have to gamble with everything he does?"

Percy lit a Lucky Strike and dropped it in the ashtray next to him. "Remember when I asked you what you like to do for fun? This is when that thing comes in handy. You've got to hang loose to make it in the boats."

Rusty had said almost the exact same thing to him on the 55.

Charlie frowned as he poured himself a cup of coffee. "I guess."

"I play banjo. The captain plays poker. Nixon builds shit like that contraption in the control room that makes ice cream that tastes like diesel. Who the hell knows what Liebold does with his time?" He chuckled. "Sticks pins in dolls, maybe. You? All I ever see you do is work. You got to blow off some steam, man. Honestly, sometimes you make me nervous."

For Charlie, the harder part of serving as XO wasn't doing his duty; it was letting it go. "How about you teach me to play a song on that banjo?"

Percy grinned. "Man, I got something better. An instrument far more worthy of an officer and a gentleman."

He pulled a shiny object from the breast pocket of his wrinkled aloha shirt.

A harmonica.

The 1MC popped. Charlie stiffened.

Moreau: *"Dive, dive, dive!"*

Percy said, "Hey, I'm teaching you. Pay attention. First thing is make a note. Anybody can do that. Pick any of these holes and blow in it …"

Charlie learned the harmonica while the submarine surfaced and dived like an underwater rollercoaster.

At last, when *Sandtiger* reached sight of the convoy's track, she dived again.

And waited for dark.

CHAPTER SEVENTEEN
BLOOD IN THE WATER

At sunset, *Sandtiger* surfaced and raced to the hunt.

West by northwest on a parallel track to the convoy, bearing 300° True.

The approach had begun. At 0130, the attack would commence.

The hours rolled past. In the conning tower, the officers and sailors performed their duties with tedious precision. For Charlie, this was the anxious time. Not just because of the imminence of action. Nor the possibility every man here might meet his maker by the end of the night.

During the approach, vital equipment broke down. Planes suddenly zoomed overhead. An escort zigged instead of zagged. Commanders with long hours between life-and-death decisions second-guessed themselves.

Charlie had experienced it during his brief command of *Sabertooth*. A leak had nearly prevented the boat from diving in the track of Japanese warships. If Jane hadn't steeled his nerve, he wouldn't have attacked at all.

Topside, the radar swiveled on its mast, sweeping the

sea for contacts. The radarman hunched in the green glow of the PPI scope. Concentric rings delineated ranges from a hundred to 1,000 yards. Bearing lines radiated from the center.

Blips winked to life on the cathode tube screen. Ships along with relative sizes, positions, and distances. An instant snapshot of the tactical situation.

As far as anybody knew, the Japanese didn't have radar. Like the bathythermograph, an amazing invention. That was how Charlie had been able to attack *Yosai* on fog-blanketed seas. With radar, the submarines might make a decisive contribution to the war—if the Navy produced a torpedo that worked.

"Radar, contact, eight ships bearing three-double-oh," the radarman called out. "Angle on the bow, starboard thirty. Speed, ten knots. Range, 18,000 yards. Two flanking escorts, six troopships in two columns of three. Targets are closing."

Percy updated the plot with his grease pencil. "They're pretty much where they're supposed to be, Skipper."

Two smaller blips, the radarman added. *Redhorse* and *Warmouth*, trailing the convoy to port and starboard.

"Looks like the gang's all here," the captain said. "Distance to the track?" The target's track being its projected course.

"Nine thousand," Charlie said.

An easy calculation. If the angle on the bow was thirty degrees, the distance to the track was one-half the range.

Moreau knew that, but captains often checked their officers and themselves by asking.

Moreau looked at the time. "We're gonna do an end-around."

In football, a trick play. The quarterback does a handoff to a receiver crossing the backfield, who then runs or throws it.

In submarine warfare, it described new doctrine pioneered by fighting captains like Moreau. If a submerged submarine was too far away from her target, she surfaced once the target had gone over the hill. Then she ran on the surface ahead of him and submerged in his track, ready to shoot when he approached.

"Message from *Redhorse*, Captain," the yeoman said.

"*Merci beaucoup*, Yeo." His lips moved while he read.

Bad news, Charlie sensed. The captain moved to the plotting table. Charlie, Nixon, and Liebold joined him there.

He slapped the paper down. "The commodore has a battle plan." Moreau swept his finger across the plot. "Rickard wants us to go far ahead of the convoy. *Redhorse* and *Warmouth* will attack, sink some of 'em, and draw off the escorts. The rest of the ships will run for Seishin. Right into us."

Charlie nodded. It sounded good to him. The survivors would be easy pickings.

"Aye, aye, Captain," Liebold said. He liked the idea too.

"Uh-huh. You say, 'aye, aye,' like I gave an order. Did I do dat?"

The torpedo officer stiffened. "No, Captain."

"Rickard didn't give me an order either. He made a suggestion. We're attacking."

"Aye, aye, Captain."

"'Atta boy." Moreau crumpled the message in his fist and left it on the table. "Charlie, call the men to general quarters."

The words galvanized the officers and sailors.

Charlie removed the mike from the 1MC call box and keyed for public address. "Battle stations, torpedo!"

The helmsman gripped the general alarm handle and pulled it out and down. The gonging alarm reverberated through the boat like a surge of electric current. Everywhere, hands rushed to stations.

Charlie readied himself for his duties as assistant approach officer. Liebold took his place at the TDC, which whirred as it warmed up. Nixon joined Percy's tracking party. During combat, he'd serve as assistant diving officer. He'd run the conning tower while Moreau and Charlie fought on the bridge.

The telephone talker said, "All compartments report battle stations manned."

"The crew is at general quarters, Captain," Charlie confirmed.

"Very well," Moreau said. "Yeo, when we're on station

and set up to attack, radio Rickard's boat. Confirm, 'message received.'"

"Aye, aye, Captain," the yeoman said.

"Oh, and tell him I said, 'Balls.'"

The yeoman walked away puzzled. The men laughed at their stations.

Charlie checked the time: 0105. He put on his windbreaker and red goggles and strung his binoculars around his neck. He was ready to mount to the bridge.

The radarman called out new bearings. The convoy steamed ahead at a leisurely pace without zigzagging. Blissfully ignorant that American submarines targeted them. Unaware blood was in the water, the sharks circling.

"Less than 500 miles from dis very spot, Tojo's snoring in his bed," Moreau said as if thinking aloud. "Dreaming about eating sushi in Washington."

Hideki Tojo had served as the Japanese Empire's prime minister since October 1941. He'd ordered the attack on Pearl Harbor. Along with Hitler, he was one of the two most hated men in America.

"He's about to get a rude awakening, Skipper," Percy said. "Least we can do to him for dragging our asses all the way out here to the other side of the world."

"Hell of a thing," the captain muttered, adrift in his thoughts.

He should wonder. Since the war's beginning, the submarines had sunk some 400 enemy ships. In exchange,

America had lost seventeen boats and the thousand officers and sailors who manned them. With aggressive new doctrines, skippers, and new technology, the tide had begun to turn.

Moreau grinned. "Dis could be a very good night."

Charlie tingled with the same sense of the sweep of history. He remembered his duties and checked the clock again. "Permission to go topside, Captain?"

"Yup." The captain pulled on his windbreaker. "I'm right behind you."

Together, they mounted to the bridge, where the quartermaster and his lookouts kept watch.

"We don't have eyes on them yet, Skipper," Smokey said.

Charlie raised his binoculars and peered into the darkness. Another cool, clear night. The seas reflected starlight and the beam of a waxing crescent moon. Across these serene waters, *Sandtiger* charged the enemy on growling engines. Batteries warm and full of juice, battle stations manned by a well-drilled crew, torpedoes ready for loading. The situation was developing quickly now. The approach neared its terminus of violent action.

One by one, the Japanese ships popped into view.

Charlie called out: "Contact!"

CHAPTER EIGHTEEN

WOLF PACK

Charlie jammed his binoculars into the target-bearing transmitter bracket. Mounted on a swivel base, the TBT sent bearing information directly to the TDC. Using it, submarine commanders could direct surface attacks from the bridge.

The leading troopships steamed dead ahead. Big black shapes on a dark gray sea. Small bow wakes. The lead escort prowled far off the starboard bow.

"Conn, Bridge," Moreau barked. "Give me a range on the lead transports."

"Three thousand!" Nixon replied over the intercom.

"Stay on the ship in their starboard column. Keep the ranges coming."

Overhead, the radar antenna spun on its mast, updating the conning tower.

"I've got the TBT on that ship," Charlie said. "Angle on the bow is port ten and opening. Speed, ten knots. He's a big ocean liner."

"That's our bow shot. We'll fire a spread of four fish. We'll hit his running buddy with another four from the stern tubes."

Charlie described the ship in as much detail as possible. The high freeboard, large single smokestack, tall masts. It stood proud on the water, a regal ship. Moving at reduced speed so the convoy's slower ships could keep up.

"*Hikawa Maru* class," the captain said. "Twelve thousand tons. Used to run the Japan-Seattle line before he got turned into a troop ferry."

Nixon: "Range, two-nine-double-oh."

Charlie turned the TBT toward the other lead ship, which had a taller prow and bridge castle. Angle on the bow, starboard ten and widening as the range closed. Moreau had aimed *Sandtiger* almost exactly between the convoy's columns.

"*Terukuni Maru* class," the captain said. "Twelve thousand tons. This is quite the operation the Japs have goin' on. Conn, Bridge! Reduce speed to one-third. Nixon, where's dat tin can to starboard?"

"Range, three-five-double-oh, Captain."

The old Momi-class destroyer steamed on, oblivious. For nearly two years, the Sea of Japan had been safe from the threat of American ships.

For the Japanese, tonight was just another routine ferry run.

"Forward room, make ready the tubes," Moreau said. "Order is one, two, three, four. Set depth at fourteen feet. High speed. Stand by on five and six."

A slight tremor vibrated through the hull as the outer torpedo doors opened.

Liebold had told the captain the Mark 14 torpedoes ran ten to fifteen feet deeper than their rating. The liners steamed with a deep draft, even deeper while fully loaded. At fourteen feet, Moreau could hit the hull under the waterline with seven to twelve feet to spare.

Nixon: "Two-five-double-oh!"

The time, 0120.

"At what range do you plan to shoot, Captain?" Charlie asked.

"When I can see the whites of their eyes. I'm gonna get as close as possible and hit 'em with everything we got. Nixon! Call for battle stations, gun action."

The alarm sounded below. Helmeted sailors poured from the gun hatch. The crew unlimbered the powerful five-inch deck gun under Smokey's direction. Others mounted the 50-caliber and 40-mm Bofors anti-aircraft guns.

Just the captain's style. Moreau planned to meet the first two ships with torpedoes. Then steam down the column, shooting at anything that moved. The weapons of choice being torpedoes, deck guns, and good old-fashioned terror.

If the boat had to dive quickly, the crew would have to leave the guns topside and lose them for good. Another gamble. With three submarines, two escorts, and a whole lot of confusion, the captain likely wouldn't have to dive until he was ready.

The ocean liners carried armaments as well. AA and 150-mm naval guns. At point blank range, it'd be hard for either side to miss.

"One-nine-double-oh!"

"After room, make ready the tubes," Moreau said. "Order is one, two, three, four. Set depth at fourteen feet. High speed."

Another tremor as the outer doors opened. Water poured in to flood the stern tubes. *Sandtiger* was now ready to shoot from her bow and stern.

Charlie kept the TBT zeroed on the Hikawa, which grew larger by the moment. The wind ruffled his hair. The engines' exertions throbbed through the hull.

"You know, Charlie," the captain said, "I expected more bloodlust from you. Thought you'd be talking about killing Japs all the time."

"I don't want to kill anybody, sir. I want to sink ships and win the war."

"Uh-huh."

Charlie hated the Japanese, but only in the general sense. Even Tojo, Hirohito, and Yamamoto were just abstractions to him. He didn't think all Japanese were evil any more than he believed all Americans were good.

What he hated was the Japanese Empire and its brutality toward countless millions. To him, it was evil and deserved destruction.

"Anyway," Charlie said, "talking isn't doing."

Moreau barked a laugh. "True enough."

Nixon: "One-seven-double-oh!"

The time, 0124.

Sandtiger advanced undetected. With her gray silhouette and very small profile, she blended into the sea. An alert lookout might have spotted her from either of the troopships. The Japanese weren't on the ball tonight, however.

"Angle on the bow, port sixty, Captain."

"Conn, Bridge. Left full rudder. Come left to oh-three-oh."

Sandtiger labored to swing her 1,500 tons as the Hikawa approached. Inside the big liner, hundreds—maybe even thousands—of soldiers snored in their quarters.

The captain conned the boat right up to the front of the Japanese formation and lined up a beautiful bow shot.

"Bridge, Conn! The escort's veering off and approaching fast."

"Very well," Moreau said.

A sharp lookout on the Momi had seen something. The destroyer's captain wanted a closer look. A future problem. He wasn't a threat, not yet.

The time, 0129.

"He's coming on," Charlie said. The Hikawa's track was only a thousand yards away. When the ocean liner's jackstaff reached his crosshairs, he pressed the TBT's transmit button. The TBT automatically sent the target bearing to Liebold down in the conning tower. "Final bearing, mark! Range, a thousand yards! Angle on the blow, port ninety! Stand by forward!"

"Set below!" the bridge speaker blared. "Shoot anytime!"

Moreau said, "Shoot!"

Sandtiger shuddered as she hurled her first shot at the liner.

"One's away!" Another jolt. "Two's away. Three's away! Four's away!"

"Forward, reload tubes one and two! Shift targets!"

Charlie wrenched the binoculars free and raced to the after-bridge TBT mounted on the cigarette deck. "New target! Stand by aft! Final bearing, mark!"

"Set below!"

Moreau: "Shoot!"

Four more kicks as *Sandtiger* loosed her torpedoes into the sea.

The two spreads reached for the unsuspecting ocean liners. Moreau and Charlie returned to the forward-bridge TBT to watch the fireworks.

At a thousand yards, *Sandtiger* could hardly miss a target that big. The liner would steam directly into their path. The momentum of his powerful engines would carry him forward, allowing the other fish to strike along his side.

As long as the torpedoes worked.

"Where's dat tin can now?" Moreau said.

"Two-double-oh on the starboard quarter, range three

thousand," Nixon said.

"Very well. Sound, stay on our fish."

"All fish, running hot, straight, and normal."

A flash yellowed the sky off the starboard beam. A moment later, a hollow boom rolled across the water. Then another.

"That's *Redhorse*," Moreau said. "Rickard got a hit."

"The escort's on a new bearing, oh-one-oh, Captain."

The Momi was speeding toward *Redhorse*.

"Beautiful," said Moreau.

Night turned to bright yellow day as a colossal roar punched the atmosphere. *Sandtiger* trembled in the aftershock.

Then the world turned black again.

"Solid hit on the port bow," Charlie said, his heart pounding.

The next torpedo exploded directly under the center mast. The third struck closer to the stern. The goliath's screws stopped. His whistle shrieked loud and long, part warning to the other ships, part cry for help.

Moreau: "Right full rudder—"

BOOM

"Mother of God," one of the lookouts breathed.

BOOM BOOM

Three successive detonations along the Terukuni's side.

Charlie grabbed hold of the gunwale as the boat rocked under him. "Three hits." A textbook attack.

Moreau chuckled. "I'll say this for Jack Liebold. He knows his way 'round torpedoes."

Another gamble that paid off.

More flashes in the distance. *Warmouth* was in action.

Whistles shrilled from every ship in the convoy. Tracers zipped across the dark as they fired in all directions.

Billowing smoke, the Hikawa groaned and listed, offering a clear view of his massive funnel. Figures swarmed across the slanting deck toward the lifeboats.

Astern, the Terukuni was dead in the water but still floating on an even keel. Klaxon alarms blared. Ranks of soldiers mustered in good order on the deck, waiting their turn to climb into the lifeboats.

"Reload completed on number one tube," the conning tower reported.

A searchlight glared across the bridge.

Seconds later, a hill of water rose from the sea close aboard.

"The Terukuni's shooting at us!" Charlie said.

"Smokey!" Moreau snarled. "Take out that goddamn gun!"

"Fire!" the quartermaster roared.

The deck gun hurled a shell at the liner and struck him amidships. The fifty-cal and Bofors guns swept the decks before focusing on the bridge. Japanese soldiers toppled where they stood or threw themselves to the sloping deck.

Charlie expected Moreau to order the helmsman to

steady the boat and ring up flank speed. Get the hell out of here in search of fresh prey. But he didn't. The boat continued turning toward the Terukuni.

Smoke blossomed as the naval gun fired again. The round tore the air overhead before punching the water with a terrific splash.

"Goddamn yellow monkeys!" Moreau raged. "Charlie, get on the TBT! We're gonna teach these Nips a lesson!"

"Aye, aye, Captain."

Sandtiger's weaponry directed its fire at the Terukuni's gun. Twisted pieces of metal and bodies flew in the air.

"Forward, make ready the bow tubes! Order is one, five, six! I'm gonna shoot our last wad at dat goddamn sumbitch!"

Another flash in the distance. Two more. *Warmouth* pounding another target.

"Meet her," Moreau said. "Rudder amidships!"

"Range, one-one-double-oh!" Charlie cried. "Speed, zero! Angle on the bow, zero! Final bearing, mark!"

He followed procedure, though the TDC wasn't necessary. The Terukuni was nearly two football fields long and barely moving. A straight shot at point blank range.

"Set below!"

"Shoot!" Moreau howled, as if possessed.

Sandtiger bucked as she pushed another 3,000-pound torpedo into the sea. Then another and another.

The deck gun crashed as it fired another shell.

Sandtiger's gun crew labored to reload with feverish bloodlust.

Nixon: "All fish running hot, straight, and normal!"

One of the escorts fired a salvo in the distance. Thunder rumbled in the deep as both destroyers randomly dumped depth charges.

This wasn't a battle anymore. It was a massacre.

The torpedoes streaked toward the liner's shattered side and detonated in three successive blasts. *Sandtiger* flinched at the detonations. The Terukuni listed rapidly as water rushed into the ship and flooded his guts. Crowds of screaming soldiers slid down the deck and splashed into the sea.

Astern, the dying Hikawa lay surrounded by a floating carpet of debris, lifeboats, and men treading water. Waves of smoke and steam rose from the groaning hulk.

"Conn, Bridge," Moreau said. "Turn us around again and send up a security detail." He turned to Charlie. "We're gonna take prisoners."

"Aye, aye," Charlie answered, exhausted.

As far as the eye could see, troopships burned, sinking. The escorts remained at least two miles away, chasing the rest of the wolf pack.

Another explosion rocked the Terukuni, breaking his back. The loudest noise Charlie ever heard. A wall of flame shot high into the air and bloomed in a massive fireball. *Sandtiger* shook in the aftermath.

"That's his boiler!" the captain shouted over the roar.

Charlie stared, transfixed, as the liner raised itself in the water before crashing back down. The hungry sea rushed up to consume it. The ship rolled with a groan, crushing hundreds of soldiers flailing in the water. Oil bled outward in an expanding slick.

Then the proud giant went down, an exhilarating and horrible sight.

THE BATTLE OF THE SEA OF JAPAN. AUGUST 25, 1943.

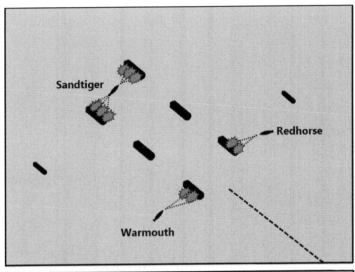

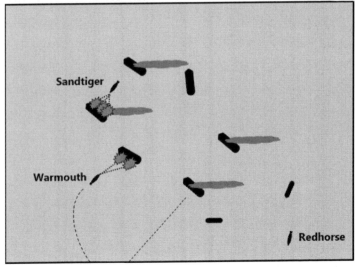

CHAPTER NINETEEN
PRISONERS OF WAR

Sandtiger reduced her speed as she waded into the floating wreckage. The security detail boiled from the gun hatch with their Thompsons, Garands, and BARs. Ready to fight, they stopped and gawked at the sight of the wreckage around the vast dying ocean liner.

Japanese soldiers and sailors huddled in crowded lifeboats. Most tread water, heads bobbing in the seas. The men in the boats turned away from their enemy. They refused even to look at the Americans they feared and disdained.

The submariners must have been quite a sight to them. Longhaired, bearded, grimy, eyes burning with hatred and a gloating sense of victory.

Charlie's ears still rang from the detonations.

"Look at 'em," Moreau said. "Look how many got off in time. The Jap Navy will pick them up by morning. Should have finished him like I did the Terukuni."

Besides its crew of some 200 officers and sailors, the Terukuni could have been carrying as many as two thousand troops packed in its rooms. Almost all went to the bottom with their supplies and equipment.

"Yes, sir," Charlie said, though he didn't begrudge survivors.

A shot rang out. Another.

A sailor cried: "They're shooting at us!"

The sailors shouldered their weapons and fired with howls of rage. The Bofors joined in, dropping rounds across the screaming soldiers. Blood sprayed in the air. The 50-cal chewed up a lifeboat and turned it into splinters in seconds.

"Cease fire!" Charlie roared. "Stop your firing!"

The men either didn't hear him or pretended they didn't.

He ran down to the deck, waving his arms. "CEASE FIRE, GODDAMMIT!"

One by one, the sailors lowered their smoking weapons, wide-eyed and panting.

Corpses floated in the water among the shell-shocked survivors. The crew had killed perhaps twenty Japanese in the brief assault.

"They fired first, Mr. Harrison," Smokey said. The quartermaster looked as stunned as the Japanese by what happened.

Charlie seethed. It was one thing to return fire against the enemy, another to shoot indiscriminately into hundreds of helpless men. The first was war, the second a war crime.

"Bag some prisoners so we can get the hell out of here!"

"Aye, aye. Come on, Artie. Give me a hand here. I see a live one."

Smokey reached down among the floating corpses. The soldier flinched away from his hands with an anguished cry.

"Stay still, goddammit! There's another one! Get him quick!"

The soldier lowered his head, gulped a mouthful of water, and went under.

The sailor reared back. "Jesus Christ. Did you see that?"

"Holy God!" another shouted.

Two more soldiers had similarly chosen death over captivity.

The sailors, full of themselves and their victory, fell silent. They regarded the suicides with superstitious awe. Who were these Japs?

"*Banzai!*" a soldier shouted from a lifeboat.

"*Banzai!*" others called out. "*Banzai! BANZAI! BANZAI!*"

Charlie spotted an overturned boat. "There. Lift it up and look under it."

The sailors crowded around and raised the boat, exposing a soldier and another man who appeared to be a sailor, one of the doomed liner's crew. They grabbed the men and hauled them dripping onto the deck.

The sailor cowered at the hateful faces glaring down

at him. He shrieked in terror. The soldier knelt on the deck, head bowed in shame.

"They attacked Pearl Harbor," the captain said. "Look at them now."

"Get the prisoners below in the forward torpedo room, Smokey," Charlie ordered. "I expect them to be treated in accordance with the articles of war."

The quartermaster looked from the captain to Charlie. "Aye, aye, Mr. Harrison. It'll be as you say."

"Secure the guns!" Moreau bawled. "Clear the topsides!"

The submarine backed away from the sinking wreck. The men secured the deck gun and stowed the machine guns.

Charlie rejoined the captain on the bridge. "Captain…the men…they—"

"Dat's four hundred sons of heaven right there, treading water. Someday, our Marines might have to fight 'em on some island. Think about dat. I wish I could kill 'em all. Because a thousand Japs ain't worth even one of our boys."

"It doesn't change what happened, sir."

Killing a thousand men in a ship earned you a medal. That was war. Killing helpless men in the water could get you court-martialed. They called that murder.

The laws of war were hard to understand. For Charlie, they boiled down to the golden rule. He fought the enemy the way he wanted them to fight him.

One day, the Japanese might capture him, and they'd remember this.

"You need to get your story straight, Exec," Moreau growled. "The boys returned fire. That's what I saw."

And that's how he'd report it to ComSubPac. Unless Charlie wanted to wash out of the Navy as a pariah, his hands were tied. "Roger, Captain."

He wasn't after justice in any case.

He'd joined the submarines to fight the Japanese Empire and find himself. Meet the man he really was. He wanted that man to be a source of pride and never shame. Shame that would follow him for life.

The memory of seeing his crew spray the Japanese with small arms made him sick in his gut. He had a feeling it would stay with him a long time.

"They got warrior culture, these Japs," Moreau said. "Think they're some kinda master race. Think their emperor is a god. They'll never love us. The only thing they respect is force. When we're done, they sure as hell will respect us."

"Yes, sir," he said. "But self-respect is important too."

The captain cut Charlie with his stare. Charlie remembered Smokey's advice: *Don't hold anything back. Attack the Japs with everything you've got.*

The captain fought the war his way. All in. To the line and sometimes across it. His former execs hadn't always gone along. One by one, Moreau banished them.

"You are treading on some thin ice, Number Two."

153

Charlie had already crossed a line himself, and there was no turning back now.

"The story is fine for the official record, sir. But if there's a next time the crew shoots at unarmed men, I expect not to be the only officer stopping it. They're going to have to live with what they did the rest of their lives."

"Point taken," Moreau said. "Now get out of my sight."

"Aye, aye, Captain."

"Hey, Charlie."

He paused in the hatch. "Sir?"

"You want self-respect?" The captain swept his hand across the vista of broken and burning ships. "Dat's where you'll find it. Nowhere else in this war. You remember dat."

CHAPTER TWENTY

TANAKA

Charlie entered the forward torpedo compartment and found the prisoners surrounded by curious submariners. Likely most, if not all, of them had never been this close to a Japanese person before. These men were the hated enemy. Propaganda had elevated them to mythical creatures, like vampires or werewolves.

He glowered at the sailors, who shrank back. "Did you search them?"

Smokey handed over wet papers. "This is all they had on them."

One of the men knelt while hugging his ribs, shivering. His eyes rolled with fear. Dressed in a white uniform, he was likely a sailor serving on the liner.

The other man wore a dark-green single-breasted tunic open over a collarless white undershirt. Trousers covered his legs. An army officer about Charlie's age.

Charlie rifled through the waterlogged papers. Identity documents, probably, along with personal letters. All undecipherable to him. In Japanese characters, the ink smeared by seawater.

The officer stared at him. His eyes flickered to the letters. Charlie handed them over. The man accepted them with a nod and began laying them on the deck to dry.

Charlie extended the rest to the sailor, who shrank back with a loud cry.

He crouched in front of him. "Take it easy. What's your name and rank? Do you speak English?"

The man didn't answer, transfixed with fear.

"You hungry? You want some food?" He mimed eating. The sailor cried out again and covered his face with his hands. Charlie mimed eating some more but gave up. "What's with him?"

The officer said in thickly accented English, "He afraid of you."

"You speak English?"

"A little. He does not."

"Why is he afraid of me?"

"He told Americans torture prisoners. Eat them."

A torpedoman grinned. "He thought you wanted to cook him, Mr. Harrison."

"I don't see the humor," Charlie growled. He held out the papers to the officer. "Give these to him. Tell him we don't eat people. It's ridiculous he believes that."

The officer spoke rapidly to the sailor. The string of harsh sentences sounded like commands.

The sailor wiped his eyes and muttered, "*Hai.*"

"The water ruined your letters," Charlie said.

"No matter. I remember words. My sword is at sea bottom. Letters all I have left to fight with."

"What's your name and rank?"

"First Lieutenant Tanaka Akio. Infantry. Army of the Greater Japanese Empire."

"Thank you, Tanaka. Smokey, write that down."

"If you wish to call me by my given name, it is Akio," the officer said stiffly. "My family name is Tanaka. In Japan, family name come first. To you, however, I am Lieutenant Tanaka."

"Good to know, Lieutenant. I'm Lieutenant Charles Harrison, this boat's executive officer. What about your friend here?"

Tanaka pulled a cloth field cap with a short peak and neck flap from his jacket and wrung it out over the deck. "I do not know him. I will ask." More rapid-fire Japanese. "Merchant marine, assistant cook, Ando Eiji."

Charlie's anger receded as the thrill of talking to the enemy asserted itself. That and the burning question: Why?

Why did they start this war? Why were they fighting? Why did they hate America so much?

Instead, he asked, "What's your unit?"

"One Hundred Eightieth Infantry Division, Twenty-Fifth Regiment."

"Why are you out here? Where were you going?"

"Manchukuo to join Kwantung Defense Army. No more fighting for us."

"No," Charlie said. "No more fighting for you."

"No more fighting for my men." The lieutenant stared at Charlie, his eyes hard black stones. "My platoon is dead in sea."

Surprising, how open the Japanese officer was to providing information. Japan had agreed to the Geneva Convention of 1929, but Lt. Tanaka might not know it even existed. The military didn't expect its soldiers to surrender; it therefore didn't train them to seek the treaty's protections.

"When you say Manchukuo, do you mean Manchuria?"

"Yes. That is your name for it."

"What was the name of the ship you were on?"

"*Roiyaru Maru*. Means, 'royal.' Like king."

"Where were you stationed before posting to Manchuria?"

"In Philippines."

Charlie frowned. "Did you serve on Mindanao?"

On Mindanao, an IJA platoon had raped Angela Lopez to death and then cut off her head. That was how Jane told it.

"No," Tanaka said. "Luzon."

"Since the beginning of the war?" He remembered Japan had been at war since 1937. "Your war against America, I mean?"

"Yes."

"Goddamn, sir," Smokey said. "Ask him if he was at Bataan."

After American and Filipino forces defending the Bataan peninsula collapsed, the Japanese force-marched them sixty miles north to a prison camp in Balanga. Eighty thousand men, already depleted by combat, hunger, and disease. The Japanese beat them at will. Drove trucks over those too weak to walk. Bayoneted others who couldn't keep up. Thousands died.

Back home, the press called it the "Bataan Death March."

"You and your friend *should* be terrified, being captured by us," Charlie snarled. "You have no right to ask for fair treatment, the way you treated us in Bataan."

"*Senjinkun*—Code of Battlefield Conduct—make surrender not allowed," Tanaka said. "My family will be told I am dead because soldiers not allowed surrendering. Surrender is dishonor. To say goodbye to country and family. To be like dog. Your men surrendered. Some soldiers treated them as dishonorable."

Charlie had made an enemy of the captain, and for what, men like Tanaka? He was angry with the captain, disappointed in himself. "The only dishonor is torturing and murdering prisoners. You dishonored yourselves by doing that."

"You do things in war. You carry them around like field pack. They get heavier and heavier. Then they become part of you. You do not plan this. It just happens. It is war. You shot my men in water with your machine guns. You are *kaizoku*. Sea robber. I am not proud of some things I did. Are you?"

Charlie stood. "That's enough for now. Smokey, I want an armed guard detailed to these prisoners at all times. Get them some dry clothes."

"Aye, aye, Mr. Harrison."

"May I ask question," Tanaka said.

"You can ask, Lieutenant."

"Why are you here? You are very far from home."

"To sink ships," Charlie told him. "Teach your people there's no point to fighting. Nowhere is safe. Our navy grows every month. You can't win this war."

"Japanese people will never be told of ships sinking. Nobody can admit you sinking our ships. We not allowed losing. You need understand."

"Understand what, exactly?"

"You cannot win this war. We fight to death, every one of us. If we have ten lives, we give them all to Emperor."

"But you don't," Charlie said and left the prisoners.

CHAPTER TWENTY-ONE

PASSING IN THE NIGHT

Sandtiger raced north until the burning ships became sparks on the horizon that one by one winked out.

The world became black again under a sea of stars.

Northerly winds stirred up swells. The submarine pitched gently on the water.

At 0230, the captain gave his executive officer the conn and went below for a few hours of sleep. Charlie scanned the darkness with his binoculars.

Despite his exhaustion, he stayed alert. Now that the battle was over, he had to be sparing with his radar sweeps.

"I don't know how you do it, Smokey," Charlie said. "You never seem to get tired."

"I'll sleep when I'm dead, Mr. Harrison."

He lowered the binoculars and eyed the quartermaster. "You all right?"

After a while, Smokey said, "It's like the man said, Mr. Harrison. It's war. Knowing those Japs were at Bataan, I don't feel much of anything."

"We're not like them."

"I heard a story about Japs pretending to surrender at Guadalcanal. Once our guys got close, they started shooting. They leave their wounded behind with a grenade hoping to take out one of our medics. Maybe we should be a little more like them if we want this war to end."

Charlie had heard the same. He'd also heard of some Marines taking ears and bones from the Japanese dead and mailing them home as souvenirs. He remembered Quiet Bill's warning this war would get nastier and bloodier the longer it went on. Charlie refused to play along. War itself may have been dishonorable, but it should be conducted with honor.

He decided to drop the subject. "Conn, Bridge. Sugar Jig, give me a sweep on the PPI."

Nixon acknowledged. A minute later, he said, "Contact."

Charlie frowned. "What sort of contact? Report!"

"Cole picked up a wavering on the PPI. He thinks it's another radar. Whatever it is, it's small. Smaller than a DD."

"A PT boat?"

"Maybe. Maybe a submarine. Target bearing one-five-oh, three-five-five relative. Range, two miles. Speed, twenty knots."

"One of ours?" Smokey asked. "The Japs don't have radar, do they?"

Charlie chewed his lip. They might. If they did have radar, they'd save it for important ships. No PT boat would rate it.

A submarine?

"Nixon, secure the radar. Come right to oh-three-five. Send a message to *Redhorse* and *Warmouth*. Find out if they're in this area."

"Aye, aye."

"And Nixon, tell the forward room to stand by."

Sandtiger breasted the swells, holding course. The range shrank to three thousand yards. Charlie ordered short radar sweeps at irregular intervals.

The target maintained its heading of one-nine-five.

"Conn, Bridge. Any word from *Redhorse* or *Warmouth*?"

"We just got a message. *Warmouth*. It's not them."

When they'd left the battle, the two destroyers had been hunting *Redhorse*. Rickard might not have surfaced yet.

Or that might be him out there in the dark.

"Call battle stations," Charlie said.

A short time later, Nixon reported, "Battle stations manned. Captain's on the way to the conn. He says to shoot the target when you're in range."

"Very well." Charlie slapped his binoculars into the TBT bracket. "Forward room, make ready the tubes. Order of tubes is one, two. Set depth at one and a half feet. High speed."

Range, 2,100 yards. He could shoot at 2,000 yards, but

it'd be a long shot. If he got any closer than that, he'd be inviting trouble.

When submarines fought submarines, the winner was usually the one that spotted the other and fired first. If the enemy detected you during your approach, he could turn the tables in an instant.

A submarine duel wasn't quite cat and mouse. It was more like cat hunting cat.

He could dive, but the fast-moving target would zip away from him before he could get a shot. He decided to tough it out. Try to get as close as possible before shooting his fish. He hoped to confirm the target was Japanese before shooting.

"I need eyes on him," Charlie growled. "Smokey, you see him yet?"

"Not yet, sir."

The window was closing. The target range would start expanding soon. He'd have to turn the boat around and give chase back toward the battle scene. An area that, in a short time, would be swarming with IJN warships.

"I've got him," the quartermaster said. "He's a submarine."

"One of ours?"

"I can't tell yet."

"Bridge, Conn! Target has us on radar!"

At the radar station, the wavering radar waves steadied on the PPI screen.

"Stand by forward! Control, stand by to dive!"

"I don't think he's one of ours," Smokey said.

A light winked in the dark.

Whoever he was, he'd spotted *Sandtiger*.

"Get the blinker gun!" Charlie barked.

"What do you want me to tell them?"

"Something. Anything. Those aren't our recognition signals. We're shooting."

Lights flashed between the submarines as they closed.

Charlie pressed the TBT transmit button. "Final bearing, mark!"

The conn replied, "Set below! Shoot anytime!"

"Shoot!"

Sandtiger bucked as the torpedo rushed into the sea. Jets of steam and phosphorescent bubbles marked its path across the water.

"One's away!"

Smokey snapped off random signals.

"Two's away!"

No response. The Japanese submarine had gone dark.

"Clear the bridge," Charlie shouted. "Dive, dive, dive!"

The men slid down the hatch. Klaxon wailing, the boat was already angling into the water.

"Hatch secured!" Smokey called out.

The captain had the conn. "Take her down, emergency! Left, full rudder! All ahead flank! Rig for silent running!"

Pressure in the boat, green board. Seawater flooded the ballast tanks. The deck tilted as *Sandtiger* penetrated the depths at a steep angle.

The crew rigged for silent running. Compartment doors slammed shut. Blowers and motors turned off. Steering and depth control switched to manual operation. Nonessential crew reported to their bunks.

Smokey counted seconds on his stopwatch the whole time. Charlie hoped to hear a boom followed by the roar of a ship breaking apart.

"Depth, forty-five feet," he said. "Control, close all vents."

"Take us to 200 feet," the captain said.

At ninety seconds, Charlie gave up hope. The enemy sub had evaded his fish.

"Depth, 185 feet," Charlie said. "Control, blow negative. Helm, reduce speed to one-third."

Sandtiger leveled off at the desired depth.

Moreau ordered the sound heads rigged out. "Sound, report!"

"He went silent, Captain," the soundman said.

Fear flickered across the captain's face. Something Charlie never expected to see.

"We just went from hunter to hunted," Moreau said.

Hours passed in silent running, but *Sandtiger* made no further contact.

The enemy submarine had disappeared.

CHAPTER TWENTY-TWO

OUT FOR BLOOD

Sandtiger surfaced and transmitted a contact report to *Redhorse* and *Warmouth*. Then she continued her northward trek, zigzagging.

Come morning, she dived.

Ocean movement. Temperature. Jettisoned garbage. Depleted diesel. Lost torpedoes. All of it affected trim, or how level the boat rested in the depths.

Charlie ordered seawater pumped from forward to auxiliary, from auxiliary to after trim. Running on only two hours of sleep, he couldn't put it together. He was "chasing the bubble."

"Any time now, Number Two," Moreau said from his lawn chair.

He wiped sweat from his forehead as if he were in combat. "Aye, aye, Captain. Control, pump from auxiliary to after trim, five hundred pounds."

"We got just two days left to kill Japs." The captain frowned as the boat shifted in the water. "Mind your bubble, Mister!"

Sensing the change in atmosphere, Percy looked from Charlie to the captain and back again. He'd seen execs wash out of *Sandtiger* after getting on the captain's bad side.

"Control, pump from after trim to sea, five hundred pounds," Charlie said.

"Five hundred out," Control reported.

At last. "We've got good trim, Captain."

"Very well. The men have had enough rest. Call 'em to relaxed battle stations. Two days. We're gonna make 'em count."

Relaxed battle stations allowed the crew their normal rotation of work and leisure time, but required the combat section remain close to stations and ready to fight.

"What's our next move, Skipper?" Percy asked.

"Back to Otaru to sink Japs." He shouted down the hatch, "Take us up to periscope depth, Chief!"

Percy nudged Charlie. "What are they like? The prisoners? I'd like to go forward and look at them myself. Prod them with a stick or something."

"The lieutenant is quite a man. Intense. He's seen a lot of the war."

"I've never even met a Jap before," the communications officer said. "And here I am killing them. Did the officer have a samurai sword?"

Charlie rubbed his eyes and yawned. "Apparently so. Lost in the sea."

"It'd be a gas to see one."

"I'm surprised how open he is about giving information. Intelligence is going to get a lot of good dope out of him."

"It's the Japanese way," Moreau cut in. "When they surrender, they break all ties with the fatherland. They don't exist anymore."

"Must be nice in a way," Percy said. "After growing up in a country run like a military boarding school. They're free men now."

"They're men with nothing to lose," the captain said. "Keep a close eye on 'em."

"The sailor seemed friendly enough once he realized we don't plan to torture and eat him," Charlie said. "He was an assistant cook on the liner." He planned to put the man to work in the kitchen, which always needed an extra pair of hands.

Sandtiger leveled off at periscope depth. The captain jerked his thumbs. He hugged the scope, slowly circling to get a three-sixty view. "Tin can, bearing two-double-oh. A pair of Zekes, far, bearing oh-eight-oh. The Japs are out for blood after what we did to 'em last night. Down scope."

Charlie expected the Japanese to respond in force, but the news disappointed him anyway. Shipping would dry up across the Japan Sea for the next few days. By the time things settled down, *Sandtiger* would be steaming back to Pearl.

But not right away. She still had time before she had

to return to base. Perhaps the captain would patrol the waters northeast of Honshu. Dangerous territory for submarines, but good hunting grounds.

He could still do some good in the war before Moreau shit-canned him.

Over the next two hours, periscope checks revealed nothing but destroyers and patrol boats swarming the surface. Meanwhile, an enemy submarine trolled the waters. As Moreau said, the hunter was now the hunted.

Their watch ended, Charlie and Percy went to the wardroom for breakfast.

Liebold sat in one of the chairs, coughing into his fist. "Good morning."

"'Morning." One day, Charlie knew, the chlorine gas would kill him.

Waldron served breakfast all around. Bacon and eggs, hot coffee.

"I heard about what you did last night," Liebold said. "Stopping the men from machine gunning the Japs. You did good, Charlie."

"Thanks." He returned Liebold's smile. At least he was off the torpedo officer's shit list. "The captain wants an exec who's just like him. I'm not that guy." He turned to Percy. "What happened to the last exec? Where did he end up?"

"Trains sailors on an S-boat at Mare Island," the communications officer said, his cheeks bulging with food. "He'll probably never fire a shot in anger again."

Charlie picked at his eggs. "Great."

"You could fight it," Liebold offered.

"I don't know." Moreau was god of this boat. If he wanted Charlie off the submarines, that's all it took. "Maybe I'm done."

"Look on the bright side," Percy said. "You could end up at Mare Island yourself. Marry that girl of yours. Work on those hobbies. Stay alive. I can think of worse fates."

"You're right," Charlie said, though he knew he'd miss the submarines. In the tedium, terror, cramped living conditions, stink, and cleithrophobia, his restless spirit had somehow found a home. "I was hoping to keep fighting, though."

"We'll win the war without you somehow, Harrison." Percy slurped his coffee. "Though many of us won't survive it."

Liebold cleared his throat. "Good morning, Captain."

Moreau entered the wardroom. "I could eat a horse." As Liebold rose from his chair, he added, "Stick around, Jack. We're gonna have us a war council."

Charlie had served under commanders who occasionally looked to his officers for advice. Moreau, who played his cards close to the chest, didn't. He leaned forward, wondering what the captain wanted to talk about.

"The Japan Sea is filling up with tin cans," the captain said, tucking into his bacon and eggs. "Trying to flush us out. We got a Jap sub in the area. We'll check on Otaru, but my guess is the marus are gonna lie low for a while."

The men watched him eat.

Moreau looked up in irritation. "So I want advice. Go."

"We made our point, didn't we?" Percy said. "We could just leave and hit them on the east coast."

"We could also try our luck here," Liebold said. "Something might turn up in two days. But I agree with Jerry. Better hunting on the Pacific side."

"Uh-huh," Moreau muttered, his mouth full of eggs. He gave Charlie the stink-eye. "What about you, sunshine? Do we stay or go?"

"I recommend we attack their destroyers," Charlie said.

"Oh brother," Percy muttered.

A dangerous idea, perhaps a little crazy. But it made sense. They'd come over 4,000 miles to maul the Japanese on their home turf. Show them that nowhere was safe. That wherever they went, American submarines would be waiting.

The destroyer was the submarine's natural enemy. Sleek, fast, and with a narrow draft, it proved hard to hit with torpedoes. Armed with big naval guns, it typically bested a submarine in a surface action. If the destroyer pinned the boat underwater, it used sonar to hunt until able to smash its prey with depth charges.

Submarine skippers typically stayed well clear of them. Perhaps not this time.

With this mission, they could show the IJN that nowhere was safe. And neither was any ship, even sub killers. The submarines would sink 'em all.

"Attack their destroyers," the captain echoed.

"Yes, sir."

"You want us to take on their destroyers."

Charlie nodded. Moreau's stern expression slipped into a grin. Then he laughed. Percy chuckled along nervously, his gaze shifting between the two men.

"Charlie, for a while there, I saw a bright future for you as commander of the *Flat-Top Desk*," the captain said. "Shooting torpedoes in the crapper."

He added, "It looks like you're out of the doghouse, boy. Let's bag us some tin cans before we head home."

CHAPTER TWENTY-THREE

ENEMIES

Charlie caught a few hours of sleep and awoke still exhausted. After coffee and a visit to the head, he read over department reports. Then a walk through the boat to make sure machines and crew had optimal function.

He was back in Moreau's good graces, but he didn't trust it. He sensed his days were still numbered. If not this patrol, perhaps the next. Charlie wanted to destroy Japanese resources without unnecessary waste of life and thereby shorten the war. Moreau's outlook had a much broader scope. He hated every one of them personally. They kill one of ours, we'll kill ten times theirs. Kill everything in sight.

Charlie doubted they'd ever see eye to eye. He felt fine about that. In a way, their styles complemented each other. One tempered the other. But the captain wanted somebody as passionate about killing the Japanese as he was.

As he passed the crew mess, the red-faced cook

waved him over. "Just wanted to thank you for the extra man. We're getting along famously."

The Japanese sailor grinned and went back to peeling potatoes.

"Glad to hear it," Charlie said. *Sandtiger* had a good cook. Despite the war, many days on patrol were tedious patterns of grinding routine. Food was the only thing to which the crew looked forward.

"I'm teaching him English, Mr. Harrison. Right, Eiji? English?"

"Fuck Tojo!" Eiji declared with a bright grin.

Charlie laughed despite himself.

"Marine are asshole!" the sailor declared.

A bad joke. When *Sandtiger* reached Pearl, the crew would hand the prisoners over to the Marines for processing.

Charlie shook his head. "Make sure he unlearns that before Pearl, Freddy."

Then he visited Lt. Tanaka in the forward torpedo room. The man sat cross-legged on one of the empty torpedo skids, surrounded by his letters. His uniform had dried. He wore his tunic buttoned to the collar per regulation. Heavy socks with a curious indent separating the big toe covered his feet.

"How goes it, Buster?" Charlie asked the watch.

"Another fine Navy day, Mr. Harrison." The auxiliaryman stood at the door with a .45 on his hip. "The prisoners are no trouble. The only excitement is the crew

176

coming around. They're curious. You know how it is."

"Lieutenant Tanaka, how are you today?"

The Japanese officer looked up from his letters and shrugged. "I am alive. Smells terrible in ship. Gives me headache."

Charlie laughed. "That's the diesel fumes. Plus the stink of sixty men. They don't call these boats sewer pipes for nothing."

"You wish interrogate me more?"

"Now that you mention it, there's something I've always wondered. What does *banzai* mean?"

"It mean, 'ten thousand years.' Wish long life to Emperor. I may ask you question? I hear men call you *hara-kiri*. Why they say this?"

"Long story. Another question for you. Why do you hate us so much?"

"I do not hate you. I grew up in Fukui Prefecture. My family grew grapes, made wine. I was in university in Kyoto to study architecture. I learn English there. I thought about girls, classes, spending money. Kyoto had dance clubs and movie houses. I watched American movies. I admired you, with your big cars and motion pictures."

Charlie sat on the edge of the skid. "How did you end up in the Army?"

"After Marco Polo Bridge Incident, we were at war with China. That was 1937. Everybody caught war fever. We looked up to soldiers as heroes. Father said Army not for me. He had government job in Kyoto. Appointed by prefect. I did not see him very much growing up. I was raised by mother, three sisters."

"Same here," Charlie said. "My dad died when I was young. My mom and three older sisters raised me."

"Father said to go to university to study. I believed he was afraid of family name dying if I killed. In university, Army officers taught how to march and clean a rifle. We bowed to portrait of Emperor every morning. War was everywhere."

In 1941, Tanaka said, he rebelled against his father and joined the Army. The IJA sent him to *Rikugun Shikan Gakkō*. Japan's counterpart to West Point. It was an exciting time. NHK, the state radio broadcaster, declared Japan would liberate Asia from the West. Create a Great East Asia Co-Prosperity Sphere for the benefit of all. Asia for the Asians!

Military life was nothing like he imagined, however. Hard work seventeen hours a day. Calisthenics, classes, homework, laundry, drilling. He learned judo, kendo, and juken-jitsu, the martial art for the bayonet. A hundred ways to kill a man. The recruits received constant abuse, beatings from the instructors. They were hungry all the time. Slowly, they became hard men ready to fight and die.

"Mother cried when I went to war," Tanaka said. "Beautiful woman. Her soul. Always singing around house. When I was little boy, she sang for me. She sang day I left. Being strong for me, though I broke her heart."

Something else they had in common. Charlie remembered leaning out the train window to blow a final kiss to his mother standing on the platform. She waved him out of sight, smiling while tears flowed down her cheeks.

Tanaka held up his wrinkled letters. "From her." He sighed. "It feels good for me to talk. I will more if you will listen."

"I don't mind. I'm actually fairly curious."

"Important that I say these things. I know I will die soon."

"We're not going to kill you, Lieutenant. We're going to put you in a camp, and you'll sit out the war. Tell me. How long did you serve in the Philippines?"

"Since beginning of occupation. Luzon. The nightmare."

Tanaka's unit moved from town to town. The engineers made a clearing in the jungle for the camp. Canvas tents, mats on the floor draped in mosquito netting. The insects ate the soldiers alive. At night, the Filipino guerillas came out of the rotting jungle. They moved without a sound, carrying their bolo knives.

"Natives hunted animals in forest. Easier to hunt us. A man would be missing. A day later, we find his head on stake."

During the rainy season, they endured weeks of downpour and mud. The soldiers raised their mats off the ground with bamboo. Hordes of centipedes crawled from their hiding places to escape the water. Racked by malaria, dysentery, and beriberi, the men shook in their beds. Feet raw with trench foot. The jungle smelling of death and decay.

In the night's darkest hours, the soldiers consoled themselves by picturing their homecoming. A massive parade honoring their victory.

"We hated natives. They could keep their islands. We wanted to go home. We hated them for living in this hell. We hated them for killing our comrades. We stopped seeing them as human. We killed them, used their women. They hated us back. Every stone, grass, and leaf in that country wanted us dead."

"Doesn't sound like Asia for the Asians to me," Charlie said. "More like Asia for the Japanese. Besides the Philippines, we didn't have anything in Asia to offer you. Why attack America at all?"

"To survive."

Charlie frowned. "Explain that."

"Father told me. He knew whole story. We need resources to feed our people and sustain our strength. We went to war with China for resources. Just like western powers did all over world and built their own empires. Your government supported China. Called us immoral for acting like European country. You refused to trade oil and materials we needed to survive."

The United States moved its Pacific Fleet from San

Diego to Pearl Harbor in 1941. That's when the Japanese decided on war with America. The nation's leaders had a choice. Withdraw from China and become dependent on others to feed their people. Or claim their destiny and take it all.

"We occupied Indochina to stop you supplying China. We offered withdrawal if you lifted embargo. You said we must withdraw from China. We could not. By then, too late anyway. We on our way to Hawaii."

"Where you launched your sneak attack at Pearl Harbor," Charlie noted.

"We did not declare war before attack. That is true. We broke international law. But you sink unarmed merchant ships. You break international law too. You are no better than we. We are no better than you."

Many Japanese people thought attacking America was a mistake. Tanaka's father held that belief, and it was the real reason he didn't want his son joining the Army. Nobody could say such things in public. The government controlled the media. The Special Higher Police enforced loyalty. In the Army, the *Kempeitai* crushed anyone who questioned official lies.

"We are same," Tanaka said. "We wanted China. You wanted us out of China. You wanted war. We started war. Now we are fighting. There is no honor in any of it. Everything else is story. A story to make men willing to kill and die. My government fooled me. You are fool to believe yours."

CHAPTER TWENTY-FOUR

GONE DARK

Plates, mugs, and silverware littered the wardroom table.

His dinner finished, Charlie slaughtered Gene Autry's "Back in the Saddle" while Percy harmonized with chords on his banjo.

"Not bad, Exec," the communications officer said when they'd finished.

He looked down at his harmonica. "I'm god-awful."

"Okay, you're terrible. But practice makes perfect."

Charlie had fallen for the instrument. Every game he played to pass the time in the submarines hinged on competition. Chess, hearts, poker. The harmonica taught him unity. Pitches in succession, each with its own duration that defined rhythm. In a way, *Sandtiger* ran like music, from its daily routines to the steady pulse of its diesels. It all worked together in harmony.

Playing helped him relax and go with the flow. You had to hang loose to make it in the submarines.

"Have you seen the prisoners yet?" Charlie asked. "The officer?"

"Yeah. Me and Nixon visited him. We just stood there gawking while he stared at pieces of paper. Like he was praying. I got embarrassed and left."

"I talked to him again. He's an interesting guy. We have a few things in common. I feel sorry for him. Trapped in the war. He wanted to be an architect."

"Don't tell me that," Percy groaned. "I don't want to see them as just like us, Harrison. The propaganda has a purpose. It's hard enough to fight them as it is."

"Well, he's free of the war now, I guess. His fight is over."

"*Exec and Mr. Percy to the conn,*" the 1MC blared.

"But not ours," Percy said. "Ours goes on and on."

Charlie checked his watch. "Almost first dog watch anyway. We're on duty."

The boat surfaced twenty minutes ago. Soon, he had to take over as officer of the watch on the bridge.

Charlie and Percy navigated the busy passages until they reached the control room. There, Spike lorded over the radio shack, radar stacks, manifold, and planes. Wheels, gauges, switchboards, and levers dominated the cramped space.

They grabbed the ladder and mounted to the conning tower. Moreau stood next to a white-faced Nixon and Liebold at the plotting table. Something was wrong.

The captain waved them over. "Flash message from *Redhorse.*"

Charlie and Percy exchanged a glance. "Sir?"

Moreau laid the message on the table. "*Warmouth*'s gone dark."

"Any idea what happened to him?"

The captain shook his head. His face was the color of ash.

Percy said, "His antenna could be damaged. Or his radio broke."

"He answered our message last night when we ran into the Jap sub," Charlie said. "That was soon after the battle—around 0200."

"We'll find out soon enough," Moreau said. "Tomorrow night is the rendezvous at Rishiri." A small island near La Pérouse Strait, their only exit from the Sea of Japan. "Rickard's already on the way."

"I'm sure Captain Shelby's fine, Captain," Liebold offered.

"No Jap alive can hurt Pete Shelby."

The two captains had been friends for years. They'd gone to Submarine School and come up through the ranks in the boats together. Same with Rickard.

"Are we still going ahead with the attack tomorrow, sir?" Charlie asked.

Moreau nodded. "Rickard's gonna join us as soon as he catches up."

"What's the plan?"

"We're gonna surface and shell Otaru Harbor from a distance of three miles."

The officers smiled as their imaginations went to

work. The sheer gall of it astounded Charlie. Shelling a Japanese port in broad daylight!

That would make an impression.

The Japanese government could lie all it wanted to its people. Tomorrow, Otaru would know the Americans had come in force.

"We'll drop rounds on the harbor until a tin can shows up," the captain went on. "Rickard will be set up off Takashima, ready to ambush the sumbitch."

Charlie nodded. The plan sounded good.

"Now get to work," the captain said. "Charlie, keep a sharp eye out for *Redhorse* topside. He's approaching bearing double-oh-five. We're moving at a slower speed, so he should be catching up soon. Don't shoot him."

"Aye, aye, Captain."

Charlie pulled on his windbreaker and mounted to the bridge with his lookouts. A northerly blew across the water. The cool night air refreshed him.

"Permission to relieve you?" he asked Smokey.

"Granted, sir. Lots of traffic up here, but we haven't had to dive yet."

The new lookouts took their stations.

Standing on the after bridge's cigarette deck, Charlie swept the southern horizon with his binoculars. Overhead, the radar made regular sweeps. Time crept as it did on the watch. The long hours gave him time to think.

Somewhere out there in the darkness, Rickard was

on his way. Tomorrow, *Redhorse* would be ready to drill holes into whatever luckless tin can the Japanese threw at *Sandtiger*. Knowing this, Charlie felt more confident in the plan.

He peered into the shades of black and gray that divided sea and sky, hoping to catch sight of *Redhorse*'s telltale smudge.

Maybe he'd find *Warmouth*.

Warmouth had cleared the battle scene by 0200 while the DDs searched for *Redhorse*. What could have happened to him? Equipment malfunction?

His mind refused to explore other possibilities. Shelby was an American, a submariner. He was one of the best submarine commanders the Navy had.

Charlie wondered if Lt. Tanaka had it right. That Japan had attacked America, but America had done everything possible to provoke it. That the war was neither heroic nor moral but an inevitable duel to the death between these rival powers. If that were true, Shelby killed and died for nothing.

He refused to believe that.

Regardless of the conflict's causes, it existed. In the end, it wasn't a fight between nations, but between men. Men connected to each other in the brotherhood of war and to the people they loved back home.

They fought for each other. More so, they fought for home. For the future. If Shelby was gone, he'd died for that.

Not for China, not for Pacific dominance, not for resources. For home.

To Charlie, this wasn't just a story. It was all that mattered.

Yellow light flickered near the horizon. The spark flared into a pulsing ball. Then it winked out.

"Conn, Bridge," he said into the bridge microphone. His heart pounded against his ribs. "Explosion, oh-seven-oh on the starboard quarter."

Redhorse had found a target.

Give 'em hell, he thought.

He counted the seconds. At eighty-eight, the muted boom rolled across the water. Sound carried about 1,100 feet per second. He estimated the explosion happened twenty miles away.

Liebold emerged from the hatch. "Flash message from *Redhorse*."

"What's the word?"

He handed Charlie the sheet of paper. "Look at this."

Charlie clicked on a flashlight fitted with a red filter. The message read:

FOR RAIDERS X CONTACT REPORT X JAP SUBM

Submarine? Rickard had tangled with the enemy submarine!

"Where's the rest of it?" he asked.

Liebold said, "That's it. That's all we got."

"Wait," Charlie murmured, trying to deny it.

The ball of light...

"The message cut off just before you called down about the explosion."

The message. Sent by a dead man. Like a warning from a ghost.

He reached for the gunwale. Steadied himself as his world suddenly shrank. He looked across the Sea of Japan's black waters.

Somewhere out there, Captain Frank Rickard and *Redhorse*'s crew tumbled to the bottom of the sea. Their final resting place, far from home.

Sandtiger was on her own.

CHAPTER TWENTY-FIVE

THE INVISIBLE ENEMY

The captain retired to his stateroom to study his Bible. The conning tower fell silent. The sailors sagged at their stations in the gloomy atmosphere.

Charlie said, "Helm, how does she head?"

"Oh-four-five, Mr. Harrison. We'll zig to three-one-five in four minutes."

"Very well."

Sandtiger raced north on all mains, hoping to distance the Japanese submarine. She zigzagged as a protection against torpedo attack. For all Charlie knew, multiple submarines had closed in after the destruction of the troopships. The Sea of Japan might be filled with lurking submarines.

Now he understood how Japanese merchants felt as they darted from port to port on a prayer. To them, the invisible undersea enemy was nowhere and everywhere.

The Japanese submarine had zeroed in on *Redhorse*'s radar pulses and made his kill. *Redhorse* spotted him, but it was too late. Rickard and his crew didn't know it at the time, but they were already dead.

Charlie pictured the lookouts calling out the incoming torpedo wakes: "Torpedoes to starboard!" Undulation in the sea. The collision alarm's grating bleat. Rickard snapping, "All ahead flank! Rig for collision!" A hail-Mary attempt to outrun the torpedo's track. The boat trembling with power. The crew in the conning tower gazing dully at their instruments, knowing they were about to die. The radioman starting his flash message to warn the wolf pack.

How long to impact? Twenty seconds? Fifteen? Ten?

What was Rickard thinking in those last moments?

"Sugar Jig, secure the radar," Charlie said.

"Aye, aye, Mr. Harrison," the radarman responded.

He pictured the enemy boat rising in the water. His decks awash, just high enough to do a radar sweep. Torpedoes on standby. Rickard had a demanding schedule to keep; he wouldn't have been zigzagging.

The Japanese skipper likely fired two Type 95 torpedoes at long range. The Navy had recently captured one. A beautiful and deadly weapon. In the years leading to the war, the IJN spared no expense in torpedo development. They knew the Americans had numerical superiority in capital ships. Both sides anticipated the IJN would whittle down American forces as they rolled west across the Pacific. Then the IJN would commit its big battleships for the final encounter.

The American Mark 14 torpedoes relied on steam for propulsion, which left a telltale trail of bubbles in the water. The Type 95 torpedoes used pure oxygen, which made them virtually wakeless. They traveled faster and farther than American torpedoes. They carried a bigger warhead and a reliable detonator.

Within a minute of detecting the American submarine, the Japanese skipper would have fired torpedoes. *Redhorse*'s lookouts wouldn't have spotted them until they were close aboard.

The same tactics had likely claimed Captain Shelby and his *Warmouth*.

"Bridge, Conn," Charlie said. "I ordered the radar secured, Jack. I'm sending up two more lookouts. For the time being, we're eyes only, so stay sharp."

"Roger that, Charlie."

"I need another two lookouts on the double," he told the yeoman.

"Aye, aye, Mr. Harrison."

Rickard was good. He certainly would have kept his head. He may have even dodged one of the torpedoes. But the Japanese skipper would have fired at least two to ensure his kill. The next shot struck amidships. Charlie knew that because of the flash and boom. The magazine had gone up in an instant. The submarine had simply exploded end to end, its twisted hulk tumbling into the depths.

Charlie didn't scare easy, but the Japanese submarine

terrified him. The way he'd surfaced just enough to deploy radar and spot his target. How quickly he'd shot his fish. How far and fast his torpedoes traveled before terminating sixty lives.

The Japanese skipper could have been firing on a friendly ship. The speed with which he'd assessed his target and fired was uncanny. How did he know the submarine he'd detected was American?

"Helm, come left to oh-two-oh," Charlie said.

"Aye, aye, Mr. Harrison."

The answer to his question was simple. The Japanese captain knew his target was American because *there were no other Japanese submarines in the Japan Sea.*

"Steady on oh-two-oh," he said. "All ahead full."

"Steady as she goes, aye," the helmsman said. "All ahead full."

No more zigzagging for *Sandtiger* tonight. The boat knifed north by northeast toward Hokkaido.

Charlie laughed bitterly at himself. After the convoy attack, the Japanese sub had acquired him on radar. While Smokey and the Japanese exchanged blinker signals, the skipper had been lining up his shot.

For *Sandtiger*, it was a simple ruse to buy time. Apparently, it had been a ruse for the Japanese as well. That skipper had been playing him right back.

Damn, he was a wily son of a bitch.

What would I do next if I were him? Charlie wondered.

Likely, he'd stick to a patrol area in central Honshu.

No, Charlie decided. *I'd move north along the coastline. Sweep the Americans out. Then back the other way, using the same tactics. Stay submerged at periscope depth, and surface just enough to conduct radar sweeps.*

That meant the submarine remained a threat to the rear in a war zone already congested with enemy warships and planes.

By morning, *Sandtiger* would reach Otaru, however. Tomorrow night, she'd run La Pérouse Strait. In all probability, the Japanese sub would never catch her.

The smart move was to bypass Otaru and make tracks for the strait. Get the hell out of this cursed sea before the net closed.

Moreau wouldn't do that. He'd made the Japanese suffer since he'd arrived. He wasn't about to head home with his tail between his legs. There was also the matter of avenging his dead comrades. Tomorrow, the captain would shell Otaru.

And unleash hell.

CHAPTER TWENTY-SIX

OTARU

Battle stations, surface action.

Morning in the Land of the Rising Sun.

The horizon burned like hot coals over Hokkaido's black mountains. The calm sea blazed red. Overhead, the paling sky glowed purple and blue, an artist's dream.

Sandtiger cruised west across Ishikari Bay. Otaru Harbor lay three miles off the port beam. Lookouts perched on her shears, watching for enemy planes.

David prepared to meet Goliath.

The helmeted gun crew tensed around the five-inch deck gun. Seated on both sides, the pointer and trainer cranked hand wheels to bear it on the target. The ten-foot barrel elevated for a 5,000-yard shot. The sight-setter corrected their aim.

A train of sailors passed up the fifty-pound cartridges. The loader shoved the first round into the breech and slammed the block shut.

"Ready to fire, Captain," Smokey said.

A line of ships lay moored at a series of sprawling wharfs in the harbor. Beyond, dozens of warehouses, buildings, and homes stacked Mount Tengu's plush green foothills.

The target: a large vessel that appeared to be a sea tender for warships.

Moreau lowered his binoculars and nodded.

Charlie roared, "*COMMENCE FIRING!*"

The gun crashed with a burst of flame and smoke that dissipated in the morning breeze. The recoil flung the hot empty shell casing into a sailor's gloved hands, which tossed it aside. The loader shoved a fresh cartridge into the breech.

Charlie glared through his binoculars. "Check fire!"

The five-inch-diameter shell tore the air in its long descent.

A geyser shot up from the bay.

"Short fifty yards!" Charlie said.

The sight setter adjusted the elevation.

Smokey yelled, "Ready!"

"FIRE!"

The pointer stomped the firing pedal. The gun bucked as it hurled another screaming shell across the lightening sky.

"Check fire!"

A decrepit freighter moored next to the tender rocked as the shell burst on its deck.

Charlie called out corrections.

"Ready!"

They had the tender zeroed now.

"FIRE!"

The long barrel spat flame with another crash. The shell whistled onto the tender's deck and exploded in a spray of debris. The gun crew cheered.

"Fire at will! Keep it hot!"

The gun crew pumped shells into the tender at a rate of twenty per minute.

Smoke rose from the burning tender as the rounds smashed into it. Anticipating airplanes, Charlie glanced at the sky. So far, clear all around.

"There's our boy," Moreau said.

Sleek and fast, a destroyer darted into the harbor. The Japanese had concealed him in a crowd of other ships behind one of the breakwaters jutting across the bay.

Fubuki-class. Two thousand tons, six 127mm guns, eighteen depth charges. An older destroyer built long before the war, but formidable.

"Secure the gun!" Charlie bawled.

"Conn, Bridge!" Moreau said. "Come right to three-double-oh, flank speed!"

Sandtiger shrieked and snarled as her engines pushed to the limit. The submarine began her turn, blowing spray and smoke from her exhaust ports.

Then she raced northwest. The Fubuki cleared the breakwaters and barreled after her with a pronounced bow wake, indicating high speed. What the submariners called a "bone in his teeth."

A puff of smoke appeared in front of his twin-mounted bow guns. The thunderous boom rolled across the bay. A terrific splash as the shells landed astern.

"Contact!" one of the lookouts called out. "Two destroyers, starboard one-one-oh, 10,000 yards and closing!"

Charlie raised his binoculars to inspect the new arrivals.

Asashios!

Twenty-four hundred tons, six 127mm guns, thirty-six depth charges. They charged toward *Sandtiger* from the open sea at thirty knots.

The Fubuki steamed in hot pursuit 6,000 yards astern.

Soon, they'd catch her in a vise.

Still no enemy planes, though Charlie knew they were coming. David hadn't just challenged Goliath. He'd ticked off Goliath's entire family.

The destroyers fired a salvo from their bow guns at long range. The shells punched the water far off the beam.

For now, the Asashios were little threat.

Charlie returned his attention to the Fubuki.

He was gaining quickly, smoke pouring from his stacks.

"Five thousand yards, Captain."

Another salvo punched the sea. Water sprayed across the deck.

The Fubuki's bow gunners were finding the range.

"Clear the topsides!" the captain roared. "Dive, dive, dive!"

The lookouts shimmied to the deck and went below. The captain followed. Charlie secured the hatch and dropped into the conning tower.

Pressure in the boat, green board. With wailing klaxons, *Sandtiger* angled into the sea.

"Helm, right full rudder!" Moreau ordered. "Battle stations, submerged!"

The fresh alarm bonged through the boat.

Charlie repeated into the 1MC, "Battle stations, submerged."

"Control, take us to periscope depth! Sound, get on that DD on our tail."

"Bearing three-oh-two. Range 4,000."

"Helm, steady as you go on oh-three-oh. All ahead standard."

"Steady on oh-three-oh, aye, Captain!"

Charlie reported, "The boat is at battle stations, Captain."

"Very well. After room, make ready the tubes. Order of tubes is one, two, three, four. Depth, two feet. High speed."

Charlie had a few moments to analyze the captain's tactics. As usual, Moreau played his cards close to the chest. *Sandtiger* had turned right. The captain intended to hit the Fubuki as he crossed the stern.

Another gamble, and a big one at that. By presenting the submarine's broadside, the captain had made her much easier to detect. By staying at periscope depth, much easier to destroy.

Sound: "Bearing three-double-oh, range 3,100!"

The Fubuki's captain raced straight toward the trap. Part of Moreau's gamble. An American submarine had invaded Japan's private sea and shelled one of her ports. Two DDs approached from the northwest. The Fubuki's skipper wanted the kill, and he had to do it fast before his brothers showed up.

A matter of honor.

"Bearing three-oh-two, range 2,250 yards!"

Sandtiger pushed to open the range to at least 450 yards, so her torpedoes would arm. A point-blank shot at the Fubuki's broadside as he passed.

"Bearing three-oh-one, range, 1,100 yards!"

Moreau jerked his thumbs. The periscope whirred from its well. The captain grabbed Charlie's shoulder and pushed him toward it. Charlie seized the handles and pressed his face against the rubber eyepiece.

Sound: "Two sets of light screws, bearing one-one-five, range 2,500 yards!"

The Asashios! They were closing the distance rapidly.

"Ignore them, Charlie," the captain said. "Focus on the target."

He swung the periscope until he centered the reticle on the hull a little forward of the Fubuki's center mast. White-uniformed sailors ran about the aft deck, preparing to dump depth charges. The prow bore the stenciled number 99. The Rising Sun flag fluttered at the stern.

"I've got him," Charlie said. "Final bearing, mark!"

Standing on the other side of the periscope, Nixon read the bearing ring on the shaft. "Bearing three-double-oh!"

"Down scope!"

The TDC whirred. The light flashed green. Liebold turned. "Set! Shoot anytime!"

"Shoot!" Moreau ordered.

Liebold pressed the firing plunger. "Firing one!"

Sandtiger jerked as the torpedo lunged into the sea.

"Firing two! Firing three! Firing four!"

"Secure the tubes," the captain said. "Sound, where are the other DDs?"

"Light screws bearing one-one-four, range 1,500 yards."

"Very well. Take her deep, emergency. All ahead flank."

The deck tilted as *Sandtiger* burrowed into the sea. Now came the wait. And retaliation. Charlie grabbed the nearest handhold in anticipation.

"All fish are running hot, straight, and normal," the soundman said.

"Rig for depth charge," the captain said. "Rig for silent running."

Watertight doors slammed shut across the boat. The only hatch left open was between the conning tower and control room, which enabled communication without the phone. The air warmed as the air conditioning cut out.

"How long?" Moreau asked, meaning how long the torpedoes had been in the water.

Liebold stared at his stopwatch. "Thirty seconds. We should be hitting soon."

The captain said, "This one's for Rickard."

"The first fish should have hit by now."

"Sound, is the target evading?"

"Target is maintaining bearing, Captain."

"I think our fish went under him," Liebold said.

The Fubuki had a narrow draft of eleven feet. The Mark 14 torpedoes tended to run as much as ten to fifteen feet deeper than their setting.

Moreau growled, "Damn these—"

BOOM

Sandtiger rocked as the shock wave struck the hull.

BOOM

"Two hits heard," the soundman confirmed.

WHUMP

BOOM-BOOM

"That's his magazine going up," the captain said.

The boat shook violently in the aftermath.

"Put it on the 1MC, Sound. I want the crew to hear his swan song."

The soundman connected the hydrophones to the 1MC, piping the destroyer's death throes over the loudspeakers.

Grinding metallic roar filled the boat. The hulk broke into pieces that grated and scraped as they tumbled through the depths. The Fubuki's final screams.

The thunder faded into a series of ghostly groans and

pops. A new sound filled the submarine. A terrible sound the crew knew all too well.

The thrash of propellers.

The Asashios were coming.

CHAPTER TWENTY-SEVEN
RETALIATION

Rigged for depth charge and silent running.

Nothing to do but wait for the attack. And survive it.

The captain dropped into his lawn chair. "I do believe I'll have my cigar."

Moreau produced one of his foul-smelling stogies and lit up, exhaling a large cloud of smoke. The acrid stench mingled with the diesel stink.

"Fast light screws, 300 yards and closing," the soundman reported.

Percy paled. "Here they come."

Officers and crew looked up at the bulkhead. Charlie wiped his sweating hands on his khaki pants and took a firmer grip on his handhold.

He hated this part. After experiencing his first depth charging on the 55, he'd wondered how any sane man could stay in the submarines.

He still wondered that.

"Fast light screws close aboard," the soundman cried. "He's making a run!"

whoosh whoosh whoosh whoosh

The men gazed dully at nothing, avoiding eye contact with each other. A depth charging was a personal experience in which each confronted his mortality.

"Splashes!"

The depth charges tumbled through the water overhead. Drums packed with 200 pounds of powerful explosive.

If you heard the detonator click, you knew it was close.

click

WHAAAMMM, WHAAAMMM, WHAAAMMM

Charlie held on as the Asashio dropped a string of seven depth charges. Deafening thunder invaded the boat, growing in volume until—

Water hammer struck *Sandtiger* like a gong. The boat shook from the concussions. Corking and paint chips flew off the bulkheads and filled the air with choking dust. A light bulb shattered and sprayed glass across the deck.

Then it was over. The men gasped and coughed in the aftermath.

"Is that all you got?" the captain said.

Charlie and Percy glanced at each other and exchanged taut smiles.

"The other target is making a run," the soundman said.

The thrash of the destroyer's screws flooded the conning tower.

whoosh whoosh whoosh whoosh

"Splashes," the soundman hissed.

Charlie barely heard him, his ears still ringing from the blasts.

click-WHAAAMMM

click-WHAAAMMM

click-WHAAAMMM

click-WHAAAMMM

Thunder rammed the submarine. The hull shuddered. Machines shook on their mountings. The deck lurched under their feet. The men moaned as *Sandtiger* rolled to port.

"Helm, left full rudder!" Moreau commanded. "All ahead flank!"

The helmsman answered. *Sandtiger* twisted in the murk, keeping her stern to the destroyers. Fleeing as fast as she could.

The destroyers switched to short-scale pinging, sniffing the deep for their quarry. The eerie echo filled the boat. The destroyers broadcast sonic energy, looking for a reflection from the American submarine's hull.

"Control, find me a thermal layer," the captain growled.

Somewhere to hide.

ping…ping…ping

The telephone talker sat up straight in his chair. "Captain! Control says—"

A man emerged through the open hatch.

Lt. Tanaka, wearing his IJA uniform.

Charlie stepped forward and froze. The Japanese officer held Buster's .45 in a tight grip. In the other hand, he clutched his sheaf of letters from home. He kicked the hatch closed and stood on it.

Moreau rose from his lawn chair. "What the hell you think you're doing, Mister?"

ping…ping…ping

Tanaka's black eyes flickered across the stunned faces of the men in the conning tower. He licked his dry lips. "You are commander?"

"If you hurt anybody with that gun, I'll goddamn hang you!"

"You are captain?"

"If you think you can escape, we're 300 feet underwater."

"I do not wish escape." The man's eyes were wild. "There is no escape."

ping…ping…ping

"This is dishonorable, Lieutenant," Charlie said. "You surrendered."

"Surrender not allowed."

"You don't want to do this. I know you don't. I can see it."

Tanaka said to the captain, "You killed my men."

PING-PING

The .45 roared with a blinding flash. Then again. Blood misted the air as the slugs ripped through the captain's body.

Moreau stumbled backward with a pained grunt. "Damn you, boy." He fell into his lawn chair, eyes glassy. Tendrils of smoke rose from his chest.

whoosh whoosh whoosh whoosh

Charlie stepped forward again. Tanaka shifted his aim and stopped him in his tracks.

"I'm going to help him. Unless you're planning to kill me too."

The Japanese officer's face froze in a rictus of terror and regret. "*Gomen'nasai.*"

Splashes overhead.

Smokey launched against the man and body slammed him against the radar console. The radarman fell out of his chair with a cry and scrambled away as the gun cracked again. The loud reports flattened Charlie's eardrums.

He ran forward—

click

WHAAAMMM, WHAAAMMM, WHAAAMMM

Sandtiger bucked at the shock waves. The jolt hurled Charlie against the plotting table. Pain shooting through his body, he rose to take in the scene:

The quartermaster pinning Tanaka with his knees. Rearing back, delivering a devastating punch to the man's face. The lieutenant's head snapping to the side, blood spraying from his mouth.

WHAAAMMM

The boat trembled then stilled. The hatch flipped

open. Spike and his sailors poured out and piled onto the prisoner.

"Secure the weapon!" Charlie said. "Smokey, that's enough for now. Take the prisoner forward. Tie him up and put a double guard on him. We'll deal with him later." He turned to the telephone talker. "Get the pharmacist's mate up here on the double. Tell him the captain's been shot."

Percy hugged the captain to shield his body from falling dust and glass.

Liebold rushed to press his hands against the captain's wounds. "Tell Doc to hurry his ass! The Old Man's alive!"

"Helm, right full rudder!" Charlie ordered.

The helmsman stared back at him like a deer in headlights. Then he snapped out of it. "Right full rudder, aye!"

Charlie said to Spike, "Are your guys okay, Chief?"

"We're fine, Exec!" Spike hung his head. "I'm sorry, sir. He undogged the door and walked straight to the ladder. We didn't have time to react."

"We'll deal with that later. Return to stations. Keep an eye on the bathythermograph."

"Aye, aye!" Spike disappeared back into the control room.

"Harrison!" Percy called. "He wants you."

Charlie knelt in front of the captain. "Hang in there, sir. You'll be all right."

Moreau winced at the pain. "Boat's yours, boy."

The deck around him glistened with blood, diesel oil, or both. Depth charges exploded far away in the deep, making the boat tremble.

"I'll get us out of this, sir."

"Swear," the captain murmured.

Charlie gripped the man's hand. "I swear."

"No." Moreau glared at him. "Kill 'em all. Swear it."

"I—I swear it, Captain. We'll kill 'em all."

Moreau didn't hear Charlie's oath. He was already dead, his face frozen in a final grimace of rage and horror.

Percy pulled himself away from the captain and openly wept, the front of his aloha shirt stained with blood. Nixon gaped at the captain, chest heaving. Doc arrived with his medical bag, but there was nothing to be done. Charlie looked up at the bulkhead, holding his breath.

The pinging had stopped.

"Fast screws on bearing oh-one-five," the soundman said. "They're moving away from us."

The destroyers had lost track of their prey.

"We're in a cold layer, Exec!" Spike yelled from the control room.

"Very well, Chief."

"Screws fading to the north," the soundman confirmed.

"Maintain this heading," Charlie said. "Reduce

speed to one-third. Secure from depth charge. Secure from silent running. It's over."

Down in the control room, the bathythermograph was scratching a downward line. By a stroke of fortune, *Sandtiger*'s right turn had moved her into a colder layer of water, confusing the enemy sonar.

Sometimes, you got lucky.

Charlie closed the captain's eyelids. "Rest now, sir."

Other times, you didn't.

CHAPTER TWENTY-EIGHT

HEALING WOUNDS

Charlie learned most of what he knew about submarine tactics from Captain Gilbert Moreau. What to do. What could be tried.

And, just as important, what not to do. What lines should not be crossed.

He didn't love the commander, but he'd respected him. Charlie would miss his steady presence in the conning tower. His leadership in combat. The entire Navy would suffer the tragedy of his death.

Sandtiger felt his loss immediately.

In the wardroom, Charlie regarded his shocked officers. "I've taken command. Our next task is to get out of the trap."

Percy wiped his eyes. "I can't believe it. The Old Man's gone."

The crew needed Moreau's command skills to get them out of the Sea of Japan alive, and he was dead.

The depth charging had given Tanaka his

opportunity. While the blasts rattled the boat, he'd snapped Ando Eiji's neck. When Buster came to investigate, the lieutenant jumped and disarmed him.

Charlie marveled at the will that it had taken to murder his countryman.

Armed with the .45, Tanaka forced the torpedomen to tie each other up. From there, a short walk through the officers' quarters to the control room. He undogged the door and asked where the captain was. Nobody told him, but their eyes flickered to the ladder leading up to the conning tower.

"We'll mourn the captain," Charlie said. "He deserves it. But first, we have to look to ourselves."

Percy lit a cigarette with trembling fingers. "I want justice. Why is that Jap son of a bitch still alive?"

"The articles of war. He'll have his trial. You'll be his judges."

Liebold grit his teeth. "We know he's guilty. I say shoot the bastard out the bow tubes now and be done with it."

"We'll follow the articles of war. The trial has to wait, though. Our immediate concern is how to get out of the Sea of Japan alive."

"What's the plan?"

"We'll stay hidden here until we complete repairs. The boat took a severe beating. Nixon?"

The engineering officer counted off the systems damaged during the depth charging. The stern firing control and tubes. The radio. The air conditioning. And the hull itself. *Sandtiger* ran about three tons heavy, waterlogged from multiple leaks and the water she'd absorbed by firing torpedoes. Ten inches of brackish water covered the main deck.

To make things worse, Tanaka's stray rounds had punched two holes in the TDC. The radar and sonar techs were pulling it apart, but Liebold didn't hold much hope for its repair.

"We can live without everything but a leaking boat," Charlie said. "Nixon, can you and your A-gangers repair the leaks by sunset?"

"Maybe," the engineering officer said. He caught Charlie's stern expression. "Probably. Yes. We'll do it."

"*Dartfish* will attack the Matsuwa airfield tonight at 0100," Charlie said. "It's our best shot at getting out. We have to be ready to cross the strait by then."

Liebold ran his hand through his greasy hair. "What if it's guarded?"

"Then we'll have to fight our way out."

Liebold sagged. "Without the TDC."

"If you can't repair it, we'll have to do it old school," Charlie told him.

The torpedo data computer had given America an edge in submarine warfare. The 1,500-pound machine automatically tracked targets and produced firing angles for torpedoes using trigonometry. The boat's radar, active sonar, torpedo rooms, bridge TBTs, and gyrocompass all linked to it.

The "old school" method, which submariners used in WWI, relied on two circular slide-rule instruments called the IsWas and Banjo. The IsWas helped determine the best course to gain a good firing position against a moving target, based on where it *is* and *was*. The Banjo was a basic angle solver for generating firing solutions. Slow and inaccurate, but it was something.

"Fighting destroyers with a Banjo," Liebold said. "Just great."

"Do or die, Jack."

Moreau had attacked a destroyer and sunk him. He might have bagged the two Asashios as well if they'd shown up just minutes later than they did. The captain proved it could be done.

"I can repair the boat," Nixon said. "I can't guarantee she can take another beating like she got, though."

"One thing at a time. Let's focus on the repairs first. Get those leaks sealed tight and the boat pumped out. Jack, see what you can do with the TDC. Percy, same with the radio. Before that, splice the mainbrace. I think we need it."

A slight smile flickered across the communication officer's face. "Aye, aye."

"Now let's get to work."

The captain had taught Charlie that with enough daring, even the biggest gambles might pay off.

Though he was dead, Moreau might get them home yet.

CHAPTER TWENTY-NINE

HONOR BOUND

Lt. Tanaka sat slumped on the deck in nearly a foot of filthy seawater.

Charlie acknowledged the watch with a nod and crouched in front of his prisoner. "How are you, Lieutenant?"

"I am alive," the man said. "Why am I still alive?"

Strong rope pinned his hands behind his back. His uniform torn, his cap gone. Bruises discolored his face. Dried blood crusted the sides of his mouth. One of his eyes had swollen almost shut.

"You murdered two men," Charlie said. "You will be tried under the articles of war."

"Ah. With proper form. It is good."

"The tribunal will find you guilty. The penalty is death."

"Of course."

"Then how is it good from where you sit?"

"Trial shows respect. Not shoot me like dog. We

will do same for you. When you are captured and held accountable for war crimes."

"You want to die? Is that what you were trying to accomplish?"

Tanaka turned away. "Dead already."

Disgraced by surrender, he believed he could never go home. As far as his country and family were concerned, he'd died in the water with his platoon.

A living ghost.

The lieutenant's head lolled as his consciousness slipped away.

Charlie grabbed a handful of his black hair. "We're not done. Wake up. My turn to ask you why."

"More interrogation," Tanaka murmured.

Charlie splashed water in his face. "Listen to me. Why did you kill them?"

The lieutenant's good eye glared at him. "I heard explosions. Thought boat being destroyed by our Navy. Had to act before I died. Killed Ando so I could take weapon from guard. Saved bullets for captain. He killed my men in water. And you. You took me from sea and brought shame on me."

"Ando was your countryman."

"He was nothing. He was traitor."

Putting on a brave face, though Charlie wasn't fooled.

He had taken a strange liking to the lieutenant during their conversations. In his mind, he'd built up the Japanese as arch villains with superhuman capabilities.

He and Tanaka had a lot in common. The lieutenant was just a typical young man doing his duty to his country, right or wrong.

In the end, however, whatever mutual understanding they'd achieved meant nothing. They remained trapped in the parts they played in this war. They never stopped being enemies.

"Can I make request?" Tanaka asked. "My letters …"

"Lost," Charlie said.

"Ah. Then I will die alone."

Charlie wanted to understand. "I thought you hated all this. You were happy to be done fighting."

"Hate this war. Yes. I did not want to kill anymore. I do not want to die. But I am soldier. Swore oath to Emperor. Surrender not allowed. You will never understand."

"I suppose I won't."

"Just as I had to try to kill you, though I do not hate you."

Charlie stood, disgusted at the waste. "I didn't hate you either, Lieutenant. But soon, I will watch you die for what you've done."

CHAPTER THIRTY

FORTUNES OF WAR

Exhausted by nearly constant combat, depressed by their captain's murder, the crew moved sluggishly through *Sandtiger*'s funereal atmosphere. The boat sweltering as the temperature climbed to ninety degrees.

Charlie worked among them, exhorting, applauding, demanding. If they wanted to survive the next twenty-four hours, they needed to push harder. If they hoped ever to see home and loved ones again, they needed to give their all.

Covered in grease, Nixon mounted to the conning tower. Percy followed.

"Repairs completed on the leaks, Exec," Nixon said.

"Well done, Nixon," Charlie said, trying not to show his immense relief. He checked the clock with its shattered glass face. "Sunset in thirty minutes."

Once they reached the surface, they could pump their bilges.

"We found our problem," Liebold said from the plotting table, where he and the radar techs had laid out the TDC's metal components. He held up a battered part.

"The resolver is damaged. And two differentials."

"Can you fix them?"

"Sure." *Sandtiger* had good machinists aboard. "But it'd take a few days. We might be able to replace the pin in the resolver easy enough. But the differentials require fine machine work. Without them, the TDC can't add."

For a moment, Charlie missed John Braddock. He'd probably fix it in a jiffy, bitching while he did it. "What about you, Percy? Any luck with the radio?"

Percy shook his head. "It's broke-dick. I'll keep working on it."

"Very well," Charlie said. "The leaks are repaired, so we're going to get moving. I'll take the boat up for a look at the surface first."

"Roger that."

"Hey, Percy."

The communications officer stopped and smiled at him. Charlie wondered if he'd helped himself to more than a single shot of the medicinal brandy.

"Yeah, Harrison?"

"Why do you always wear those loud aloha shirts?"

The smile faded. "I bought one in Hawaii and was trying it on when the captain called battle stations. We sank a converted whale factory. I thought the Old Man would chew me out after. Instead, he told me I had to wear them all the time. He said it brought him luck."

Charlie nodded. "Carry on then. We're going to need all the luck we can get." He leaned toward the open hatch. "Control, take us up to periscope depth!"

"Aye, aye, Exec!"

Sandtiger had to surface soon. If she didn't, she'd run out of air and power. She also needed to find a safe place to pump the water from her bilges. The pumping would create a visible slick on the surface.

"Sound, do you hear anything up there?"

"Light screws, bearing oh-nine-one. Range 3,000 yards. No pinging. Not sure what it is. Sounds like a PT boat."

Sandtiger leveled off at sixty-five feet.

"We'll take a quick look at him. Up scope!"

He crouched and rose with the periscope shaft, slapping down the handles. The sea undulated in the wind. Cloudy skies. A pair of seaplanes, 4,000 feet elevation, far. A distant landmass, which was Hokkaido.

He turned the view toward the ship the soundman detected.

Charlie cried, "*Battle stations, torpedo!*"

The battle stations alarm bonged through boat. The galvanized crew rushed to man their stations.

"Down scope! Helm, swing us around! Steer to one-eight-oh!"

"Aye, aye!"

"What's going on?" Liebold wondered.

"Jack, get the Banjo!" He pulled down the 1MC microphone and said, "Mr. Nixon and Mr. Percy to the conn!"

Percy arrived and took his station at the plotting

table. "What did you find?"

Nixon followed. "Here, Exec!"

"I need you as assistant approach officer," Charlie said.

The engineering officer brightened. "Aye, aye."

"Up scope!"

He swung the periscope until he'd centered his crosshairs on his prey.

The biggest submarine he'd ever seen.

More than 300 feet long. KD type, from the distinctive faired metal sail that housed its conning tower. I-class. Dark gray with the upper parts of the sail painted black. No hull number.

A banner had been attached to a frame on the sail. A red sun on a white field.

"What did you find?" Percy repeated.

"I'm looking at the submarine that sank *Redhorse* and *Warmouth*. Right at his meatball."

Percy gasped.

This was the guardian of the Sea of Japan.

"Sound, keep those bearings coming," Charlie said.

"Oh-nine-two, oh-nine-two and a half, oh-nine-three—"

No zigzagging.

Dressed in white uniforms and Donald Duck caps, sailors lounged on the bridge and cigarette deck. Smoking, laughing. They were a proud and happy crew after destroying the American invaders. Mission accomplished, they were headed to Otaru for a few weeks of liberty.

"Give him twelve knots. What do you think, Sound?"

"Two hundred RPM. Yeah, about twelve knots."

"Angle on the bow, port fifty! Down scope!"

The officers gathered at the plotting table. Percy sketched it out for him.

"He'll cross our bow at 1,500 yards. We'll have a straight bow shot."

Sometimes, you got lucky. Sometimes, you hit the jackpot.

Charlie intended to exploit this break for all it was worth. But he needed to get closer and reduce the range. The only way to do that would be to increase speed. At nine knots, he could shorten the range to 1,100 yards.

If he ordered flank speed, he'd drain what little battery power he had left. If he missed, the response would be fast and furious. He'd have to engage the submarine while being trimmed heavy. Ships and planes would arrive shortly after.

And he wouldn't be able to stay under much longer. In just a few hours, the air would run dangerously thin, and the battery would start to flatline.

The clock read 0515. Sunset in another twenty minutes. The safe move was to run for the strait. Get the hell out of here.

"Helm," he said, "how do we head?"

"One-eight-oh, Mr. Harrison."

"Keep her so. All ahead flank."

"Steady as she goes. Increase to flank, aye, Mr. Harrison." The helmsman selected flank speed on the annunciator, which responded with a bell chime.

Jack opened his mouth but closed it. He understood the risks but knew better than to say anything.

"Forward room, make ready the tubes," Charlie said. "Order of tubes is one, two, three. Set depth at two feet. High speed."

The forward torpedo room acknowledged. The soundman called out fresh bearings. The situation remained more or less static. The Japanese submarine cruised east at twelve knots. The American submarine moved south toward him.

The torpedo outer doors thudded open.

Charlie keyed the 1MC. "Attention. This is the exec. We spotted the Jap sub that sunk *Redhorse* and *Warmouth*. We're on an intercept course. We'll make a submerged attack. This one's for our comrades. This one's for Moreau."

It was time OPERATION PAYBACK earned its name. Time for him to keep his promise to Moreau and kill 'em all.

"Up scope!" There the submarine was, blissfully ignorant he was being hunted. "Bearing, mark!"

Nixon read the value on the bearing ring. "Oh-nine-four!"

Liebold wheeled a disc on his slide rule. "Roger."

"Range, mark!" Charlie said.

"Range, 2,000 yards!" Nixon said. "Speed, twelve knots!"

"Roger," Jack acknowledged.

"Angle on the bow is port sixty-five! Down scope!"

Liebold lowered the Banjo. "We're looking good for that straight bow shot. If you shoot at the right time, he'll run right into our fish."

"Forward room, torpedo angle is zero degrees," he said. "Up scope! Final observation."

He centered the crosshairs on the submarine's gray broadside. Right under the big meatball on her metal sail. "Stand by forward! Final bearing, mark!"

"Oh-nine-five!"

Liebold: "Set! Shoot anytime!"

Charlie hesitated. Something about this felt wrong. Those sailors out there were submariners. Men just like him.

He actually pitied the Japanese skipper. The IJN hadn't warned him about a third American submarine in the area. That or the skipper decided the Americans had left.

You made one mistake, let your guard down once, and you were dead.

The fortunes of war.

"FIRE ONE!" he cried.

Liebold pressed the plunger on the firing panel. The boat kicked as the first fish left its tube and lunged toward the enemy submarine.

After eight seconds: "FIRE TWO!"

Compressed air pushed the second torpedo from the boat. Its propellers cranked the warhead through the water at forty-six knots.

"FIRE THREE!"

Even one hit would do the job. Submarines didn't sink nice and slow like a big surface ship. The boats carried little reserve buoyancy. They sank like rocks.

"All fish away!"

"Down scope! Forward, secure the tubes. Stand by to dive. Sound, stay on our fish."

"All fish running hot, straight, and normal, Exec."

"Very well."

Nothing to do now but wait as the torpedoes sped toward the target. The conning tower fell into a tense hush.

Sound: "Oh-nine-five, oh-nine-five, oh-nine-five and a half—"

The enemy submarine held its course. The seconds ticked past.

"How long?" Charlie asked.

Liebold held the stopwatch. "Forty-five seconds."

Not long to go now. "Up scope."

The submarine cruised serenely toward Ishikari Bay. Sailors on the cigarette deck stiffened in shock as they spotted lines of bubbles reaching for their boat. Several pointed at the nearest wake. One cupped his hands and shouted a warning.

"The first fish went right under him," Charlie said with disgust.

So did the second.

The third nailed him amidships with a heart-stopping roar.

"One solid hit!" the soundman said.

"The detonation broke him clean in half," Charlie told the excited crew. "He's going down."

Smoke and dust hung in the air. The bow reared and sank in a terrific fountain. The stern followed at an angle, consumed by the roiling foam.

Sandtiger bucked as thunder rolled against her.

Charlie waved Smokey over. "Here, take a look."

Smokey grinned at the view. "That's for Captain Moreau, Jap bastards."

"I didn't thank you, Smokey," Charlie murmured. "If it weren't for you, Tanaka would have shot me too."

"Sink a few more Japs, and you'll have earned it, sir."

The quartermaster stepped aside. The officers took turns at the periscope to see the results of their work.

When Charlie took the scope back, nothing but debris floated in an expanding oil slick. He circled three times to check again for threats. Clear water and skies. The sun bled into the horizon. Night was coming quickly.

"Down scope. Stand by to surface." He took the mike from the 1MC. "Attention. This is the exec." He swelled with pride. "Scratch one Jap submarine."

Across the boat, the crew cheered. Charlie had given

them vengeance for *Redhorse* and *Warmouth*. Vengeance for Moreau.

Now it was time to make the run for home. They just had to make it through La Pérouse Strait.

CHAPTER THIRTY-ONE

HOME RUN

Sandtiger cruised on the surface thirty miles west. There, she pumped her bilges. Then she struck north, her radar sweeping the sea for threats.

Ten miles out from La Pérouse Strait, blips appeared on the PPI.

"Radar, contact!" the radarman called out, his face bathed his cathode tube screen's green glow. "Three ships, bearing one-five-oh. Range, 19,000 yards."

Charlie studied the screen over the man's shoulder. "Destroyers?"

The man turned, his face shining with sweat. "They sure look like it to me, Mr. Harrison."

"Are they using radar?"

"Just their active sonar. Long-scale echo-ranging."

The green cursor line swept around the circular plot. Sakhalin to the north, Hokkaido to the south, the ships in between. Clustered near the edge of the screen, the blips jumped position as the plot updated. Then again.

Sentries, guarding the strait. Weaving back and forth.

They straddled a six-mile stretch of water that marked the channel through the minefields. Each jump brought the blips closer to the center of the screen as the range closed.

Dartfish had shelled Matsuwa's airfield at 0100, an hour ago. Whatever damage he'd done, it hadn't been enough to budge these tin cans.

Sandtiger was alone. Mauled. Trapped in a hostile sea.

No choice now but to fight her way out.

He said, "Clear the topsides. Rig to dive."

The diving alarm sounded.

Charlie had wanted to command his own boat ever since he first set foot on the S-55. There, J.R. Kane had taught him patience and to think analytically about combat.

Wait for the right move. Then strike with everything you had.

Nixon shouted commands to seal the boat and get her ready to dive. The engines cut out. The main induction banged shut.

"Pressure in the boat, green board," Nixon reported. "Ready to dive in all respects, Exec. The boat has 296 feet under the keel."

As the boat grew closer to the destroyers, the depth under the keel would shrink to 200 feet. She wouldn't be able to go deep to evade depth charges. She'd have fewer thermal layers in which to hide.

"Very well," he said. "Dive."

On *Sabertooth*, Charlie had tasted command. A boat

full of refugees, a deliciously distracting Army nurse, and one hell of an opportunity to sink a heavy carrier that attacked Pearl.

On that boat, he'd served under Bob Hunter, who'd taught him the role luck played in combat. That the most successful commanders made their own luck.

Now he held the reins of command again, and he didn't want them. So tired, he just wanted to let somebody else make the decisions.

What was the best move here? How could he improve his luck?

"Flood safety!" Nixon barked. "Flood negative!"

Sandtiger slid into the sea.

The destroyers blocked La Pérouse, *Sandtiger*'s only way out. She needed to cross the strait on the surface or else perish in the minefields.

She could strike west and evade the Japanese for another month before her fuel ran out. The IJN would bottle up the straits, but after things settled down, perhaps they'd send the ships elsewhere.

No guarantees on that, though. The IJN knew a third American submarine prowled their private sea. They wouldn't rest until they sank her. They might send more ships into the sea searching for her.

Things looked bad now, but they'd only get worse.

"Control, take us to periscope depth," Charlie said.

Another option was to simply glide through the sentries, surface, and make a run for it. Hope to lose the destroyers in the strait's pea-soup fog. There, radar would give *Sandtiger* a decisive advantage.

She'd have to make the run across miles of water with no fish left in the after room and three fast-moving tin cans on her tail. A no-go.

The only option was to attack. Fight her way through the blockade.

Three destroyers, six torpedoes. He had to make that add up.

It added up, all right. It added up to *Sandtiger*'s annihilation.

He'd always known the odds were on this being a one-way trip. Still, there was a chance at survival, however slim.

"A submarine attack is a lot like high-stakes poker," Moreau once said. *"You start with a stack of chips. Concealment, surprise, torpedoes, battery power, air. Your very lives. You gamble them one at a time to win."*

"Helm," he said. His voice sound stretched and thin. He cleared his throat.

The helmsman stared at him. "Sir?"

Whatever fears he had, he couldn't let them show in front of the men.

"Some men fold early. Others, if the pot is big enough, they gamble it all."

Charlie said in a firm voice, "Call the men to general quarters."

Battle stations, torpedo!

CHAPTER THIRTY-TWO

ALL OR NOTHING

Battle stations manned. Rigged for silent running. Six torpedoes loaded in the bow tubes. *Sandtiger* glided through the depths at three knots.

Six shots, three tin cans.

Every fish has to count, Charlie thought.

The math was simple.

Three of the six have to hit, or we're dead.

Even with a TDC, fire control remained an inexact science, which was why commanders fired a spread at their targets.

Right. We don't have the fish to deliver a good spread per target.

Sandtiger also didn't have a working TDC.

Destroyers are damned hard to hit.

If he missed, the destroyers would react with devastating force. They'd push her under. Then they'd smash her to pieces in the shallow waters.

He shook his head. *Enough of that*. It was do or die. They had no choice. "Rig for depth charge. Up scope."

Charlie crouched, pulled down the handles, and rose as the periscope extended from its well to break the water above. Hugging the scope, he circled twice.

He spotted the sleek destroyers in the dark. Brought the nearest ship into view, an Asashio-class destroyer. Very likely one of the tin cans that gave *Sandtiger* a pounding off Otaru. "Acquiring target, Asashio. Bearing, mark!"

"One-seven-five!" Nixon said from the other side of the periscope.

"Range, mark!"

"Fifteen hundred yards!"

"Angle on the bow is starboard seventy. Speed, twenty knots. Down scope."

The periscope whirred back into its well in the deck.

Liebold turned the discs on the Banjo. "Set."

Sound continued to call out target bearings: "One-seven-five, one-seven-five, one-seven-four and a half—"

Charlie wiped sweat from his grimy, bearded face. "Nixon, you ready?"

"Roger, Exec."

"Jack?"

The torpedo officer fidgeted with the Banjo. "Ready."

"Stand by, forward. Up scope. Final observation."

Charlie focused the crosshairs under the Asashio's center mast. In the darkness, he made out faint Japanese markings on the hull. The Rising Sun flag waved at his stern. His deadly twin five-inch bow and stern guns stood ready to fire.

"Final bearing, mark!"

Liebold finished his firing solution. "Recommend spread of twenty and twenty-four degrees."

"Nixon?"

The engineering officer tilted his head as he ran the numbers in his mind. "I concur, Exec."

"Forward, set gyros by hand. Two-oh and two-four degrees."

"Gyros set," the telephone talker confirmed. "Torpedoes ready to fire."

"FIRE ONE!"

Sandtiger bumped as she released her first torpedo.

After eight seconds: "FIRE TWO! Down scope."

"Forward confirms both fish are in the water," the telephone talker reported.

"About a minute to impact," Liebold said.

The soundman turned his sound head control wheel to acquire the torpedoes moving through the water. "Both fish are running hot, straight, and normal."

"Very well," Charlie said, breaking out in a fresh sweat.

Liebold counted the seconds. "Twenty-six, twenty-seven, twenty-eight—"

"Up scope." Charlie centered the periscope's view on the destroyer.

"Fifty-five, fifty-six, fifty-seven—"

A blinding incandescent flash, followed by a roar that shook the boat.

The destroyer shuddered, his back broken and his screws stopped. The ship bent inward. Depth charges tumbled from their racks and exploded against the bridge castle.

"He's lighting up like a firecracker," Charlie said.

Fire raged at the center of the ship, which began to sink, shooting gouts of burning diesel oil. The bow and stern reared out of the water until almost vertical, flinging spray and debris. Then both plunged into the boiling sea.

"Scratch one destroyer." Charlie swung the periscope. "Contact! Another DD's coming at us with a bone in his teeth. Shifting targets."

The destroyer charged at the exposed scope, bow wake foaming like a mad dog rushing for the kill. A Fubuki, smoke pouring from his stacks.

"We're spotted," he said. "He's zigging."

The Japanese skipper played it safe, weaving as he ran at the submarine.

"Bearing, mark! Range, mark! Speed, thirty-five knots!"

Liebold feverishly worked the Banjo, sweat dripping down his face.

Again—bearing, range, angle on the bow, and speed— until they had a general idea of the Japanese skipper's pattern.

The bow guns boomed. Charlie didn't see where the shells landed. "Stand by forward!"

He couldn't shoot farther than 1,200 yards, or the

destroyer would have time to dodge his torpedoes. He couldn't shoot less than about 500 yards, or the torpedo wouldn't arm. The timing had to be just right.

The destroyer's V-shaped prow grew larger until it filled his view. The bow guns fired again. The submarine rocked as the shells struck the sea close aboard.

"Jack…"

"Wait!"

Range, 750 yards and closing.

"I need a firing solution now!"

Jack gave it. Nixon concurred. Charlie told the forward room to set gyros by hand. Then he gave the order to fire.

"Three's away!"

"FIRE FOUR!"

"Four's away!"

Charlie's knuckles ached as he gripped the periscope handles.

Sound: "Fast light screws, bearing two-four-five!"

The third destroyer, fast approaching. The sea around the protruding periscope lit up clear as day. A searchlight.

Just a few more seconds…

The zigging Fubuki's bow exploded in a fireball.

"We hit him! By God, we hit him!"

Sound: "Fast light screws, close aboard!"

Charlie screamed, "Take us down to 180 feet, emergency! Dive! All ahead flank!"

whoosh whoosh whoosh whoosh

Sandtiger bore into the water, heading directly under

the sinking destroyer. The crew looked up in terror, faces glistening with sweat. Above, the warship shrieked and groaned as he sank.

CRACK-BOOM

The men flinched at the loudest sound they'd ever heard. Then another and another. The destroyer's magazine or boilers had exploded. Maybe both. On the surface, the dying DD shuddered, buckled, flew apart.

The water roiled around the submarine as the first pieces plummeted to the bottom. Within seconds, it was raining metal. Metallic howls and groans echoed through the submarine from all sides.

Almost through the gauntlet. Depth, seventy-five feet.

Sandtiger shuddered as something big struck the forward deck and slid away into the deep with a grating shriek of metal.

"Jesus Christ," Liebold said.

Then they were through.

Charlie took a ragged breath. "Sound, try to get on that last DD."

The sea behind them churned as the Fubuki's final remains tore through the water on their way down. The thunder faded to a ring in Charlie's ears.

Sound: "He's short-scale pinging!"

"Where the hell is he?"

"I've got him. Bearing three-five-five. Range 1,600 yards."

"What's our depth?"

"A hundred feet," Nixon said.

"Bring us back to periscope depth. We're going to sink the bastard."

The battle wasn't over until *Sandtiger* had sunk all three warships. That was the only way to get through the strait.

"Sixty-five feet and holding, Exec!"

"Stand by forward. Up scope!"

Blinding white light. A dark V-shaped prow with a pronounced bow wake.

"He's spotted our scope! Bearing, mark! Range, mark!"

Liebold shook his head but produced a firing solution. The telephone talker relayed the manual gyro settings to the torpedo room.

"Come on, come on," Charlie growled.

The destroyer grew larger by the second.

"Torpedoes ready!"

"FIRE FIVE! FIRE SIX! Down scope! Right full rudder! Dive! Take her down, emergency!"

The two torpedoes streaked from *Sandtiger* toward the destroyer. The boat groaned as she turned in the water and angled down.

"Fast screws, close aboard!" the soundman cried. "He's starting a run!"

whoosh whoosh whoosh whoosh

The torpedoes had missed.

"How deep are we?"

Nixon checked the gauge. "Eighty feet, Exec!"

Not enough.

"Splashes!"

click

WHAAAMMM, WHAAAMMM, WHAAAMMM!

The hull buckled at the blasts. Bulbs burst. Gauges shattered. Overhead piping cracked and sprayed cold water across the room. Men screamed as the lights went out and the concussions hurled them across the room.

Charlie held on with both hands in the dark, his feet leaving the deck as the boat listed heavily to starboard. Something struck in him in the forehead over his right eye. He dropped to the deck and landed on a body. Alive or dead, he didn't know. Then the boat's roll swept him across the sloshing deck.

The emergency lighting popped on. Dust and insulation swirled in the weak light.

Charlie stood among the coughing men. He touched his throbbing forehead. His hand came away wet with blood. "All compartments, report damage!"

BOOM

The blast tossed him like a ragdoll. He slammed against the TDC and flopped to the deck gasping for air. *Sandtiger* heeled over, stopped for a moment by the explosive force. Then she rolled again, her crew tumbling with her.

Liebold shook Charlie's shoulders. "Get up! We're being bombed!"

Christ, the Japanese were throwing planes at them now.

244

whoosh whoosh whoosh whoosh

Pinging steadily, the destroyer made another run. The soundman should have reported this, given them some warning. But his station sat empty, his equipment smashed.

It didn't matter. They were done. What did Liebold want from him? He just wanted to be left alone and sleep.

Liebold shook him again. "Charlie!"

He wagged his head. Covered in several inches of filthy seawater, the deck tilted under him. The boat remained angled down. "What's our depth?"

Liebold helped him to his feet. "One-seven-five. We're going down fast!"

The boat was out of control and heading to the bottom. With the hatch closed and dogged, there was no way to talk to the control room except on the XJA or JA circuits. Wet and battered, Charlie splashed through the oily water toward the telephone talker's station.

click

WHAAAMMM, WHAAAMMM, WHAAAMMM!

Sandtiger shook like an earthquake. Charlie stumbled and lost his footing on the slippery deck, landing hard on his knee. He cried out as pain shot up his thigh. He lunged and grabbed the headset.

"Control, Conn! Get control of your—!"

BOOM

Charlie's vision flared white.

He awoke propped against the bulkhead, his legs

245

underwater and his chest warm with his own vomit. Blood poured over his left eye, half blinding him. Nixon stood under the overhead piping with a wrench, feverishly working to close a valve. Liebold dragged a body through the water. Percy, wearing one of his loud aloha shirts, was raving into the phone.

"Pump the water out!" he screamed. "Pump the fucking water out!"

Sandtiger couldn't take much more than this. She might be dying already. A one-way trip. Charlie had wondered what Rickard thought about in those last moments before the Japanese torpedo blew him back to God. Now he knew. His entire life passed before his eyes.

His mother nibbling a single piece of dry toast while she watched her children eat. One of his sisters cleaning behind his ears with a washcloth. J.R. Kane moving a chess piece, "Check, Harrison." Evie sipping soda through a straw while she talked about their future, the home they'd build, the beautiful children they'd one day have. Jane undressing in his room at the Royal Hawaiian, taking her time, staring him in the eye with a slight smile as if daring him to look away.

Rusty reading aloud from the letter he wrote his wife on the eve of the Battle of Blanche Bay: "I love you. I'm sorry. Be happy."

Charlie thought about Evie. *I'm sorry—*

Sandtiger shook again, groaning as another string of depth charges pounded her hull. The men staggered at

246

the hammer blows, shouting to each other. The radarman sat on the deck, screaming with his hands over his ears.

Charlie slid from the bulkhead onto his side in the brackish water. The boat bucked again. The deck had more or less leveled out, he realized. Trimmed heavy, the boat had an up angle. The planesmen had taken control of the planes and stopped *Sandtiger* from slamming into the sea bottom.

They still had a chance.

The pinging faded in volume as the destroyer completed his run and turned about for another go.

Charlie hauled himself to his feet, dripping blood and water. "Helm." He coughed hard into his fist, ribs flaring with pain. "Helm! How does she head?"

Nixon answered for him. "Oh-oh-five, Exec!"

"Right full rudder!"

The helmsman cowered against the bulkhead.

Charlie splashed through the water until he stood over the shaking sailor. "Helm, mind your rudder! Return to your station!

The sailor crept back to his post. "Right full rudder, aye!"

"Take us into the strait! All ahead flank!"

The officers stopped and stared at him.

"That's suicide!" Percy said. "Helm, belay that order!"

Charlie clenched his fists. "Mr. Percy, shut it, or you're relieved!"

"It's crazy—"

"Silence!" Charlie roared. "Helm, head for the strait! That's a goddamn order!"

The helmsman gaped from Percy to Charlie with wild eyes. "Aye, aye!"

"Why?" Percy pleaded.

"You sure about this, Charlie?" Liebold asked.

Charlie said, "It's our only chance."

Sandtiger limped toward the minefields. Row after row of horned mines moored to the bottom, swaying in the murk.

"Control, periscope depth," he ordered into the headset. "Spike, put fresh men on the planes. We'll need to hold depth at exactly sixty-five feet for the next thirty miles. Not a foot deeper."

The chief hesitated before saying, "Aye, aye."

The conning tower fell into a tense silence, the men holding their breath. The pinging faded as she entered the strait. The boat tingled at distant explosions, fresh planes dropping their payloads onto the sea.

Then no sound except for the loud ringing in their ears.

Liebold was the first to break the silence. "I'll be damned."

Sandtiger cruised at periscope depth in La Pérouse Strait.

When the boat had entered the Japan Sea, Charlie theorized the IJN mined the strait at a depth of seventy feet. The strong current caused the mines to dip at least several feet, providing more room between the submarine's keel and the mines.

The torpedo officer shook his head in amazement. "How did you know?"

"I didn't," Charlie said. "It was just a theory."

And the biggest gamble of his life.

CHAPTER THIRTY-THREE
FINAL RECKONING

Sandtiger's crew held the general court-martial in the mess hall. As trial judge advocate, Charlie faced Tanaka at one of the tables. Acting as jury, Percy, Liebold, Nixon, and two ensigns sat at another table. Smokey wrote everything down to produce a court record. Off-duty crewmembers crowded the rest of the room and the outside passageways, craning their necks to see.

"First Lieutenant Tanaka Akio, 25th Regiment, 180th Infantry Division, Imperial Japanese Army," Charlie intoned. "You, a person subject to military law, stand accused of murder of two men. Lieutenant-Commander Gilbert Moreau of the United States Navy and Ando Eiji of the Japanese merchant marine. Do you understand the charges against you?"

Tanaka rubbed his wrists, worn raw by his bonds. "*Hai.* Yes."

"You are entitled by the articles of war to counsel. I understand you wish to waive this right. Is that correct?"

"Yes."

"Let the record show it. How do you wish to plead then?"

"I am guilty."

The crew growled as one. A sailor called out, "Goddamn right you are!"

"Silence!" Charlie snapped. He turned to the tribunal members. "There will be no need for you gentlemen. I am ready to pronounce the court's judgment."

He fixed his stare on Tanaka. The lieutenant put up a brave front, but he trembled as he awaited his sentence.

This man had murdered Captain Moreau in cold blood. He'd snapped his countryman's neck as a ruse to escape.

At the same time, he was pitiable. Take the uniform and everything it represented away, and he was just a terrified man. In his mind, he was simply doing his duty to his nation. A duty he'd perform to the very end, though he detested it.

Charlie didn't like it either. A strange thing. He'd killed hundreds, if not thousands of men by ordering torpedoes launched. Now here he was, discomforted by the prospect of sentencing a single man to death.

Percy was right. The propaganda served an important purpose. Nameless, faceless demons were far easier to fight than real, flesh-and-blood men. The more nightmarish and monstrous the enemy, the easier he was to kill.

Charlie said, "Lieutenant Tanaka, you are hereby sentenced to death. The United States Navy will punish you. It's up to God to forgive you."

The crew's throaty cheers filled the boat.

"SILENCE!" Charlie roared. "Do you understand the punishment?"

"Yes."

"Do you have anything to say before punishment is carried out?"

"I told you I would die soon," Tanaka said.

"That was your choice. Smokey, remove the prisoner."

Tanaka's stony expression faltered. "Wait. Please."

"Yes?"

"Please let me die in daylight. I want to see my country one last time."

"Very well. Punishment will be carried out topside at dawn. Court adjourned."

Sailors hauled Tanaka away. Exhausted, Charlie slumped with his head supported by his hands. The execution he ordered was simple justice, a necessary act. Still, he wouldn't feel joy at the man's death.

A horrible waste, all of it.

His head throbbed under the bandage. His ribs ached with each breath. Pain lanced from his knee to his hip as he hauled himself to his feet.

Little time to sleep and heal. Too much to do to put *Sandtiger* to rights. By tomorrow, she'd be free of the Sea of Okhotsk and back in the Pacific. From there, she'd cruise to Midway to finish repairs and replenish her provisions.

Meanwhile, the boat was a shambles, held together by sheer stubbornness. Every system damaged. The crew labored to repair leaks, restore function, and jury-rig fixes that, with luck, would see them arrive safely at Midway.

Percy approached. "Hey, Exec?"

What could it be now? "Yeah?"

"I just wanted to say sorry I tried to contravene your orders. No excuse, Exec. It won't happen again. I lost my shit back there. Okay, that's my excuse."

"Percy, we have a lot of work to do," Charlie said. "I've got bigger things on my mind right now. If we make it back to Oahu alive and intact, I'll remember to tell you not to do it again or I'll keel-haul you. Sound good?"

The man grinned. "Sounds fine, Exec."

"Carry on."

As he reached the passage, Charlie called out to him.

Percy turned. "Yeah?"

He said, "Splice the mainbrace, if any of the bottles survived the battle. After what we went through, better make it a double ration."

The communications officer sketched a salute. "Aye, aye!"

Charlie returned to his stateroom and stretched his battered body on his bunk.

Then Smokey was shaking him. "Dawn soon, Mr. Harrison."

Eyes burning from exhaustion, he checked his watch. Two hours gone in a wink. He accepted a cup of coffee from the quartermaster. "Thank you. You know, you might try to catch some shuteye yourself."

"When I'm dead, sir. When I'm dead."

Charlie changed into a fresh uniform and mounted to the conning tower. "Attention, sections two and three," he said over the 1MC. "All hands, bury the dead." He flicked the switch to OFF. "Helm, reduce speed to one-third."

Sandtiger wasn't out of danger yet, not by a long shot. Holding the funeral now was a risky move. So was holding Tanaka's execution at dawn. But the crew had lost more than they'd won and needed this closure. They'd given their all and would be asked to give far more by the end of the patrol.

Charlie mounted to the bridge under a sea of stars obscured by cold thinning fog. Lights glimmered in the distance, Russian trading ships plodding toward Vladivostok. The AA guns stood manned and ready to fire.

Percy, Liebold, and Nixon joined him on the bridge. The crew filed out under a doubled lookout detail perched on the shears. Some limped, others wore bandages, a few carried their arms in slings. They all looked grim.

Then three bodies. The Japanese merchant marine Ando Eiji, a casualty of Tanaka's private war. Electrician's mate Zack Tyson, whom everybody called "Granny" due to his many years in the submarines; he'd died of electrocution while restoring power to the boat's forward section.

And Captain Moreau, sewn up like the others in a sailcloth burial shroud.

The crew stood at parade rest while the burial detail carried Moreau's body to a waiting stand. The big captain's feet protruded overboard. The sailors draped the Stars and Stripes over him.

Charlie said, "Unto Almighty God, we commend the soul of Lieutenant-Commander Gilbert Jerome Moreau. Captain of the *Sandtiger*. The best of the best. Thanks to men like him, we'll see an end to this war."

He nodded to Nixon, who bawled, "Firing party. Present arms!"

A line of sailors stiffened, Garand carbines held in front of their chests. The burial detail tilted the stand. The Stars and Stripes waved as Captain Moreau slid and splashed into the sea.

"Fire!"

The guns crashed as one. Again. Then a third time.

After the other two burials, Charlie dismissed the men. The firing party stayed behind with their Garands. The officers remained on the bridge.

Smokey brought out Lt. Tanaka and positioned him on the deck. "Do you want a blindfold?"

"No. I want to see my homeland."

"Suit yourself."

Charlie said, "Jack, give this to him."

Liebold stared at him, puzzled. Then shrugged. He descended to the deck and gave the wadded-up ball of paper to the Japanese officer. Covered in oil, the handwriting illegible, reduced to rags.

Tanaka looked up and smiled. Charlie nodded.

The sun peered over the eastern edge of the Sea of Okhotsk. Beams of light spread into the darkness. Tanaka's last view of the rising sun.

The lieutenant squinted into the darkness to the south. Out there, Hokkaido, just a black smudge on a dark gray horizon. His homeland.

"It's time," Smokey said.

"It is time," Tanaka agreed.

"Any last words?"

"I did my duty. Now you must do yours."

"More than a duty. A pleasure." Smokey called out, "Ready!"

The sailors readied their carbines. All of them volunteers for the firing squad.

"Aim!"

Tanaka turned away from Japan and gazed again at the rising sun.

"Fire!"

The pop of the carbines filled the air. Tanaka slumped to the deck in a puff of smoke.

Moreau's death, avenged at last.

CHAPTER THIRTY-FOUR

HOMEWARD BOUND

Land ho!

Sandtiger plowed the waters west of Oahu under a clear blue Pacific sky. Charlie stood on the bridge, eyes glued to the sliver of land on the horizon.

His officers grinned at the sight. Almost home.

"I hope they got our messages," Percy said. He'd repaired the radio, but while it could send, it couldn't receive.

Liebold said, "It'd be pretty sad to survive all that only to be sunk by one of our own planes with a trigger-happy pilot."

Charlie lowered his binoculars. "We'll find out soon enough."

He glanced at them with pride. Liebold, the genius who'd rigged the torpedoes and given Charlie accurate gyro settings under pressure. Percy, who'd taught him the value of letting go. Nixon, socially inept but unflappable in combat. And Smokey, the veteran who tirelessly held the crew together.

At Pearl, the boat would receive more repairs. The crew would enjoy a few weeks of hard-earned rest. Then boat and crew would unite again. Return to the war against a stubborn enemy that refused to give up.

A band would be playing on the dock. Apples, ice cream, and mail for the returning heroes. Captain Cooper would be waiting to receive Charlie's report, and what a tale he'd hear. *Sandtiger* had accomplished the impossible. Still, with everything they'd lost, it didn't feel quite like victory.

"Smokey," he said. "It's time to raise the colors."

"Aye, aye."

"And Smokey? Have a man bring up a broom."

The quartermaster grinned. "Will do, Mr. Harrison."

Sandtiger was returning with fresh patches on her battle flag and all torpedoes spent. It was custom to tie a broom to the shears, indicating a clean sweep. She deserved the honor. Six ships sunk, 31,000 tons.

He hoped she'd receive a unit citation.

The sailors hoisted the Stars and Stripes. Then the battle flag with its brand new patches. Two transports, three destroyers, one submarine.

After that, the Jolly Roger.

Another look through his binoculars. Oahu larger now. Weeks of peace and quiet. Charlie smiled at the prospect of a long hot bath. A hot meal. A stiff drink. An hour or two practicing the harmonica. Then a full night of uninterrupted sleep in a soft bed.

No Evie or Jane waiting for him this time. While peaceful, the next few weeks promised to be long and lonely.

Smokey interrupted his thoughts. "Problem below, Mr. Harrison."

"What is it?"

"The starboard engine."

"Very well," Charlie growled. "Nixon, you'd better come too."

He went below and followed the quartermaster aft.

The crew roared at his arrival in the mess hall. Forty bearded sailors in blue shirts and dungarees. Charlie took it all in, stunned by the display. The quartermaster patted his shoulder.

Spike belted out, *"For he's a jolly good fellow!"*

The crew joined in. The cook brought out a massive cake. Between chocolate frosting landmasses, *Sandtiger* ran a vanilla strait to freedom.

The men finished to loud cheering.

Spike grinned at him. "You did right by the captain, Mr. Harrison, and you did right by us. We just wanted to say thanks for bringing us through."

Charlie stammered as the men cheered again. He didn't know what to say. "This is…I'm proud…" He shook his head and smiled. "Thanks a lot, fellas."

He cut the cake, and the cook served pieces all around. The men dug in. Nixon handed him a big piece and a fork. Charlie took a bite. It was delicious.

Smokey patted his shoulder again. "Told you you'd make out all right."

Charlie just nodded. He didn't have the words.

The yeoman approached. "Mr. Liebold says he spotted a PC boat on the starboard bow, flashing recognition signals."

"Thanks, Yeo." He took another bite and set down his cake. "Duty calls."

Charlie mounted to the bridge.

Leaning on the gunwale, Percy winked at him. "Fix that engine, did you?"

"It's never run better."

The communications officer beamed at Oahu. "Don't know about you, but the minute I get back, I'm going to get my kicks in a way that would put Caligula to shame."

Liebold said, "Permission to bring her into the harbor, Exec?"

"Sure, Jack." He'd certainly earned it.

Sandtiger cruised into the channel. The excited crew boiled out of the submarine and crowded the deck.

Charlie was happy too, but for different reasons. In his last two war patrols, he'd returned to medals and promotions. This time out, he'd earned something worth a whole lot more. The respect of the crew.

He was a submariner now, though and through. He'd finally arrived.

Soon, *Sandtiger* would be home. As for Charlie, he was already there.

WANT MORE?

If you enjoyed *Battle Stations*, get ready for the next book in the series, *Contact!*, scheduled for publication in spring 2017. In this episode, Charlie takes part in a mission to support the invasion of Saipan, culminating in the Battle of the Philippine Sea.

Sign up for Craig's mailing list at CraigDiLouie.com to stay up to date on new releases. When you sign up, you'll receive a link to Craig's interactive submarine adventure, *Fire One*. This story puts you in command of your own submarine, matching wits with a Japanese skipper…

Turn the page to read the first chapter of *Contact!*

CHAPTER ONE

RUNAWAY TRAIN

Lt. Commander Charlie Harrison stood on *Sandtiger*'s bridge as Captain Harvey conned her out of Pearl. Today, the fifteen-man Relief Crew 202 of the USS sea tender *Proteus* would determine if she were seaworthy.

They were healing, man and submarine, and getting to know each other again.

Seven months ago, *Sandtiger* limped into Pearl with new scars and a broom tied to her shears. Sailors crowded the wharf and watched in silence as the battered boat warped to the dock. Word had gotten around. Disaster in the Japan Sea. The sailors thought they were seeing a ghost ship, this sole survivor.

Then they'd cheered loud enough that ComSubPac heard it in his office.

Sandtiger exited the harbor mouth for her shakedown, trailing black smoke. For Charlie, a moment of vertigo as she seemed to shrink, facing the vast Pacific.

Lt. Morrison said, "We're underway, Captain."

"Very well. Dismiss the maneuvering watch."

"Aye, aye."

"Set a course for two-seven-oh."

"Setting a course for two-seven-oh, aye," the first officer echoed.

Charlie smiled at the tedious but important routine. It felt like home just as being back at sea did. The submarine's engines pulsed like a strong and healthy heartbeat as she found her bearing.

Sandtiger had survived, but it had been a near thing. Her wood decking and steel superstructure warped and broken. Commutator short circuits in the starboard main motor. The electrical and steering system turned fickle. Drain pump sparking. Multiple leaks, including one through the stern torpedo tubes.

Charlie feared she'd be scrapped, but she'd gone straight to shore repairs. Struck by the loss of three fighting captains, ComSubPac wanted *Sandtiger* back in the thick of it. Vice Admiral Lockwood couldn't bring back Moreau, but he could the man's martial spirit.

The repairs took longer than expected. By the time the engineers declared her ready for sea, Charlie had completed Prospective Commanding Officer (PCO) School at New London. He'd returned hopeful for a posting to new construction and had been happily surprised to find *Sandtiger* waiting for him.

He glanced over his shoulder at Waikiki Beach. A crowd of men stood on the white sands. The regular ship's company, wishing her the best. Somebody raised a drink in salute, probably Lt. Percy. Like Charlie, they belonged to her.

He hoped he would become her captain.

Ahead, the Pacific beckoned. The tropical sun burned across gentle swells, creating a golden road. A destroyer—the USS *Grant*, a four-gun Benham—emerged from the glare. Lt. Morrison called out the arrival of their escort.

Charlie smiled again with a fierce joy. Nothing could ruin this moment.

"Did you miss me, Mr. *Hara-Kiri-san*?"

He started at the familiar grating voice. Looked up to see John Braddock, one of the four lookouts, grinning down at him from the shears.

"Keep your eyes on your sector," Charlie said on reflex.

He thought about the heavy thumping *Sandtiger* had taken on her last patrol. How good Braddock was at fixing equipment, even if he seemed even more skilled at ruining everything else.

Charlie added, "And you know what, I actually did. What are you doing here?"

"Right now, I'm on lookout."

"I mean what are you doing on a relief crew?"

"Staying alive by staying as far away from you as possible, sir."

Just as Charlie remembered, Braddock made *sir* sound like *asshole*.

Captain Harvey lowered his binoculars and glanced

up at the big sailor before fixing Charlie with a glare. Charlie shut up and kept his eyes forward, his face a practiced mask of professional sullenness. Captain Squadron Commander Rich Cooper had said he could tag along but only if he stayed out of Harvey's way.

Lt. Morrison threw him a furtive wink. Brash and looking far too young to be first officer, he struck Charlie as a go-getter chafing to transfer and see combat before the war ended. Stationed on sea tenders, relief crews manned submarines during shore repairs. They provided a valuable service but never faced the enemy.

Sandtiger continued to reach from the shore, making way on growling engines. The *Grant* paced her to starboard. Oahu's bright coastline and lush green mountains receded to a blur. Her prow knifed the swells.

Morrison broke the silence with a report. Depth under the keel, 500 feet.

"Clear the topsides," the captain snarled.

The men hustled down the ladder to the conning tower. The last man called out he'd secured the hatch. The klaxon blasted twice as the captain gave the order to rig for dive. Wedged into a corner of the crowded room, Charlie listened to the boat's hum, felt it along his spine.

The iron lady appeared healthy and strong.

"Dive, dive, dive!"

"Maneuvering, Conn," Morrison said. "Stop the main engines. Switch to battery power."

The big generator, which powered the electric motors

that turned *Sandtiger*'s four propellers, switched from engine to battery power.

"Rig out the bow planes."

The blades thumped as they extended into the sea.

"Manifold, close the main induction," the first officer said.

The valve banged shut. The Christmas tree glowed green across the board, signifying all hull openings secured.

"Pressure in the boat, green board, Captain. All compartments ready to dive."

Harvey scanned the conning tower as if to confirm everything was in order. His eyes settled on Charlie, followed by a frown. He clearly didn't like an officer from the regular ship's company being here. Probably felt he could give the boat her proper shakedown without some hotshot looking over his shoulder.

"Very well," the captain said. "Planes, take us to ninety feet."

The brawny planesmen turned their wheels in opposite directions. Bow planes rigged to dive, stern planes angling the submarine.

Morrison: "Control, open all main vents."

The manifoldmen opened the vents to allow seawater to flood the ballast tanks, draining the boat's buoyancy.

Harvey would dive to the boat's test depth in stages, checking her trim and that there were no leaks. After that, steep ascents and descents to give her a thorough trial.

Angles and dangles. Then he'd fire dummy torpedoes at the *Grant*.

The men leaned as *Sandtiger* tilted for her dive.

Charlie stiffened. Something was wrong.

The deck kept tilting.

His heart leaped into his throat as *Sandtiger* surged forward at a steep down angle and plummeted into the depths.

"Control your planes!" Harvey cried in surprise.

A wrench clattered and slid down the sloping deck. Charlie gripped a handhold, watching the captain.

"Passing ninety feet!" Morrison said, his brashness gone.

Harvey grimaced, trying to figure out the problem. Out of control, *Sandtiger* bolted toward the bottom like a runaway train.

The depth gauge needle spun crazily as she sank.

Face taut and pale, Morrison held on with both hands to keep from sliding down the deck. "Passing 150 feet!"

"Recommend blowing the ballast tanks!" Charlie called out.

Harvey looked around wildly, saying nothing.

"Blow the goddamn tanks, Captain! All back emergency!"

The captain gave him a blank stare, his face glistening with sweat.

"Now or we're done, Captain!"

"Passing 200 feet!"

The boat trembled as she hurtled toward her test depth.

"Surface, surface, surface!" Morrison screamed.

The first officer had taken the conn without declaring he was doing so. The desperate crew obeyed without question.

The helmsman yanked the alarm handle. "Surfacing, aye!"

"Control, blow the main ballast tanks!"

Harvey snapped out of his funk and roared, "Hard rise on the bow and stern planes! All back emergency!"

"Aye, aye!"

All eyes were on the captain now, while he stared at the depth gauge.

"Passing 300 feet!"

The orders came too late. *Sandtiger* was passing her test depth and entering pressures that could warp her steel hull.

Then deeper until the heavy waters crushed her like an egg.

Harvey shouted fresh commands to pump water from the amidships trim tank out to sea. The boat shook as her engines fought to check her descent.

Depth, 350—

The hull groaned and popped as the surrounding water pressed against it.

Charlie's mind flashed to the Japan Sea. Nixon laboring to close a spraying valve with a pipe wrench.

Liebold dragging a body through the brackish water covering the deck. Percy screaming into the 7MC circuit.

Evie standing at the edge of a pier at Mare Island, waving a red scarf.

Four hundred feet.

Sandtiger shuddered as if she were coming apart—

Then Charlie felt the change.

The boat's descent was slowing. No longer sinking like a rock.

Manifold had punched a bubble into the bow and main ballast tanks. The deck began to level out as the bow rose.

Sandtiger lurched again and shot up fifty feet. The crew worked hard to get her under control and keep her moving toward the surface.

Morrison took a ragged breath. "We're out of it, Captain."

"Something's wrong with this boat," Harvey growled.

He glared at the submarine that had flatfooted him. Scanned its dials and levers as if this mere inspection might derive the cause among thousands of moving parts.

His glare settled on Charlie as if he'd found his culprit.

Charlie didn't care. He'd just survived another brush with death; the captain's embarrassment and anger meant nothing to him. In any case, he had a bigger worry on his mind right now.

What was wrong with *Sandtiger*?

ABOUT THE AUTHOR

Craig DiLouie is an author of popular thriller, apocalyptic/horror, and sci-fi/fantasy fiction.

In hundreds of reviews, Craig's novels have been praised for their strong characters, action, and gritty realism. Each book promises an exciting experience with people you'll care about in a world that feels real.

These works have been nominated for major literary awards such as the Bram Stoker Award and Audie Award, translated into multiple languages, and optioned for film. He is a member of the Horror Writers Association, International Thriller Writers, and Imaginative Fiction Writers Association.

Learn more about Craig's writing at:
www.CraigDiLouie.com

24798871R00160

Printed in Great Britain
by Amazon